LOVE ACROSS TIME

SOUTHERN SISTERS FATED MATES

BOOK ONE

T.C. LYNNDALE

Cover Design by H.E. Gober

Edited by Lacy Chantell Publishing

Proofread by Michelle Healy, PA

ISBN (ebook) 979-8-9937771-0-8

ISBN (paperback) 979-8-9937771-1-5

Version: 1.25-11-10

DEDICATION

To all the grown-ups who wished they were magical as children.
You were and you are.

And...
To my sister, without whom I would not have actually done this.

And...
To my real-life book boyfriend, the most amazing hubby I could
ask for.

CONTENT WARNING

This book contains sexually explicit content and open-door romance scenes. It also includes themes of grief and loss (including parental loss and the death of a lover) and family revelations about a biological father.

Please read with care if these topics are sensitive for you.

PROLOGUE

HYACINTH

"We're having a party, Tansy! You're turning thirty. This isn't twenty-nine, it's thirty!" Azalea animatedly argues as she walks into Hornbuckle's Bar beside Tansy. I follow along behind, and we wave to Rod working the bar as we jump into the seats at 'our' high-top.

"Usual?" Rod hollers over the crowd.

"Yes," we say in unison.

"Please let us plan a nice party. This is a milestone birthday. We have to celebrate you," I say, looking at both my sisters before sliding off the high-top chair. "Don't y'all say a word about the birthday plans until I get back. I can't hold it anymore."

Speed walking to the bathroom, I say a quick 'Hey,' to Tucker sitting at the end of the bar. I think about how much of our adult lives we've spent right under Rod's watchful eye. Once in the bathroom, I grin. On an old piece of metal with a picture of an old boat, it says, Washroom - Keep it Clean, or

1

Face the Consequences. It makes me laugh every time. I don't know why Rod won't let me spruce up this place. It could be so much cuter in here, even if he just let me add some flowers.

Sighing, I finish up and head back to my sisters.

Tansy stares at her glass of Crown and Coke, clearly frustrated, absentmindedly stirring it with her straw. Azalea has a margarita with a chaser of tequila and looks around the bar with my rum runner waiting beside her. I love that Rod knows exactly what we want. I guarantee a chicken sandwich is coming for Tansy. He'll surprise Azalea since she changes her order every time. And I'm the only one he makes a pepperoni pizza for. Technically, it's not a dish on his menu. If anyone else asks, he simply points at the menu and walks away. He's such an old grump.

I stop to say a quick 'Hi' to Rod. He nods his head, acknowledging me, while still serving his customers. That simple nod is equivalent to a full conversation with anyone else. Rod hands Tucker his beer as I walk by.

"Hey Tucker. How are things?" I ask.

"It's been dry lately, so we could use more rain for the crops. I would take having to run the sprinklers over those storms from a couple years ago any day, though," he says.

I wince. "Well, I hear the forecast is calling for rain in the next couple of days, right?" I tap his shoulder as I turn to go back to our table. His grunt the only response.

I remember those storms and what caused them. It's so hard knowing how we affect those we care about without even trying. Mental note: *Don't mention this to T. She would get upset.*

Returning from the bar, I see our food ready at the window. Glancing around, it seems as if the server hasn't been back to this side of the room for a while, so I grab the tray and carry it to my sisters. The moment I sit, I notice

Tansy is still nursing her first drink while Azalea is ready for her second. Of course, Rod makes sure we all have a glass of water to go with our booze. He always tells us, 'You need to stay hydrated with your beverages.'

Azalea is so excited about the wings Rod put in for her; she forgets about her empty drink entirely. Settling back into my seat, I ponder how to bring up T's birthday again. She needs something special to celebrate and have some fun. Life hasn't been easy for her, and she always puts us and her son, Hawthorne—or even that stupid Henry James Daniels II that she finally divorced—before herself. Or at least, she used to. Dr. Douche is long gone, thank you very much. She deserves better than him; it's not like he was her FateBond or anything. Now it's just Hawthorne and us that she puts before everything else.

Okay, Hy, focus. How do we get T to allow us to do something just for her?

Erika and her husband, Gary, come into the bar and immediately head in our direction. Erika excitedly talks with Azalea; her face lit up with a smile.

"Thank you so much for telling me about those herbs! They have worked miracles! I haven't had one migraine, or even a headache, in two full weeks."

Gary nods along and adds, "It's like before the accident. I can't believe it either. I really wish we had thought of talking to you sooner."

Z beams with pride. "I am so glad you feel better! Now, if you run low, just let me know. Come on by The Garden anytime."

As I sip my drink, I think about how much I love watching people be amazed by Z. She always makes it seem like no big deal and has a profoundly positive impact on the community. Just as many people come into The Garden to see her as they do to buy flowers. My thoughts drift. Maybe at some point, we should add another section just for her, like an apothecary of some sort.

As Erika and Gary say their goodbyes to find their table, I'm still pondering how to get Tansy to let us throw her a party. There won't be a good way, so I decide to just go for it.

"T, listen, we really want to throw you a party. Something calm and simple, but nice. We can invite just a few people over and have dinner." Clouds gather in her eyes, and her lips part, but Azalea jumps in.

"Not another nice party. Ugh. No, we need to have an actual capital 'p', party. Let's have some fun. I'm sure Rod would get us a keg."

"No, no, no," T says through a clenched jaw, her grip tightening around her sandwich. "We can have dinner here at Horney's just like every other Thursday. No party. No gathering. No big to-do. I don't want all of that. As it is, Hawthorne will have dinner at the Daniels, and I don't want more time away from him. Just drop it."

Z and I exchange glances, realizing we won't win this debate. The oldest sister overrules or something. Still, we'll celebrate her, but it'll have to be low-key like Tansy wants.

CHAPTER 1

HYACINTH

I'm at the back of the car gathering up all the birthday goodies. Balloons, a small dessert box, T's present, a card, all while my purse is draped across my neck. I can make it in one trip; I will not have to come back out. I arrived a full hour before our normal dinner time to make it perfect. Tansy won't be too mad, right? We are still at Horney's—just making it more about T for her birthday. Besides, how can we not have dessert for her birthday? Seriously, who doesn't want a birthday cake? Only Tansy. Instead, I went to the bakery that has the good double chocolate brownies she loves. With everything in hand, I head inside to get set up.

Since it's still early, Hornbuckle's Bar is pretty empty. Rod looks up and chuckles as I try to get through the door. I'm sure I look a sight with my sparkly light blue dress and heels with this big pile of stuff. He makes it over to me just as the present is slipping.

"Had to do it in one trip, huh?" he asks.

"One trip or bust! And besides, Rod, I wouldn't want to deprive you of the opportunity to make fun of me. Er...I mean, save me."

He laughs, "Like you would actually let someone save you! I would never make fun of you, Hy."

We laugh as we head toward the table I picked out for tonight. Rod moves the little metal 'reserved' sign from the table.

"Do you really think that's necessary?" I ask.

"Well, I figure since I only have an excuse to use these things occasionally, I might as well. Besides, it's always just for my girls."

Rod rushes around and grumbles to himself as I finish making sure the balloons and flowers are perfect. He keeps glancing at his watch. It has definitely seen better days with the old dry leather and crack on the watch face. I wonder if there's a story there.

I take the brownies up to the bar and ask if I can keep them in the kitchen until we're ready for dessert. Rod grunts as he preps for the Thursday night crowd. Ever since I convinced him to have a karaoke night once a month, it's been so much busier. Our weekly dinners are louder, but honestly, I think it's perfect.

After taking the brownies to the back, I stop at the counter and corner Rod to figure out what's going on. "Rod, you're grumpier than usual. What's up?" I ask.

Gruffly, he replies, "Nothin'. Got it covered."

"Okay, so that means there is something. Come on now, seriously, what's going on?" I ask.

He huffs, "I'm gonna have to find some new help, that's all. It's not a big deal. I just know tomorrow is gonna be a long fucking day."

I've never considered what it might take to be a waitress,

but I have to help Rod. Plus, I have a new cute linen dress that would be perfect to fit the overall ambiance—not that Rod thinks there is an ambiance in his bar. Meadow's Garden isn't busy now, and that's more Tansy's anyway. Z has her tonics and such that she makes, but I don't have anything that is just for me. Before I can think about it another moment, I blurt. "I can do it."

He stops restocking the Truly's—which he begrudgingly started carrying after we began having ladies' night—and glances at me. "Nope."

"Listen, I could use a change of pace. Really, you would be helping me out. The Garden isn't busy right now since the big Valentine's Day rush is over. Tansy & Z can handle it." I give him my best customer service smile.

"Just until I find someone," he relents.

I don't know why I'm so excited about being able to help him out. Well, maybe I do. Lately, it seems like I'm always in a bad mood, and I'm thinking it may stem from working at The Garden. I love working with my sisters, but I constantly have to remind myself not to be a grumpy goose!

Working at Horney's will be new and exciting. Rod will be behind the bar, thank the heavens. I mean, I could probably pour a beer. Hopefully, I won't have to find out. My brain keeps spinning and spinning like a hamster on a wheel. If I stay organized, it can't be that bad. It's just a lunch and dinner service. It'll be fun, and Rod has always been such a solid rock in our lives. It'll be nice to do something for him for a change.

Azalea walks in a few minutes before Tansy is expected to arrive. She looks like a million bucks, dressed for big city party instead of our little town. Her purple dress hugs her curves to perfection. She pulled her auburn hair up tonight, which I know means she doesn't want it in her way while she dances. I can't help but notice the sparkle in her hazel eyes from the excitement over the celebration and the treats we have in store for Tansy.

"The store was steady today, but nothing crazy. Tansy started out in a bad mood. Dr. Douche called to 'wish her a happy birthday and tell her he hopes she is happy in this hick town.' Like, what does he think? She was never gonna leave here." Z talks a mile a minute.

Before I can even get a word in, she's already at the bar. "Rod, oh Rod, my most favorite bartender, especially on my sister's birthday! Can we please get one Pirate's Booty with three straws?" Rod raises an eyebrow and sighs. "YES!" she exclaims as she skips back over to our table. She loves the opportunity to have a party and drive Rod crazy with her antics.

Pirate's Booty is served in a fishbowl with blue curacao and white rum, fresh fruit, and pirate coins gracing the bottom of the dish. Rod tops it off with soda water for that bit of fizz that makes it so refreshing, and not too strong. It's sitting on the table when Tansy walks through the door. My Amazonian sister pulled out all the stops with her smoky eyes and long, wavy hair. Only she can pull off a black wide-leg flowy pantsuit and heels.

She immediately starts shaking her head in mock disapproval, but she's smiling. I know she'll have a good time; she needs to loosen up a bit first.

"Thank you so much for making my 30th so special." Tansy whispers as she hugs us both. "I'm sure this is of your doing?" Her gaze lingers on the massive three and zero metallic pink balloons announcing her age.

"And Z, that has to be your doing!" she says as she points to the fishbowl.

I can't help but smile as Azalea jumps up and down. "T, I'm so glad your birthday falls on karaoke night!" Waving her phone, she convinces one of the other patrons to take our picture with the Pirate's Booty.

Tansy pretends to be mortified and tries to look serious. "I will not be participating in karaoke. I will have one sip of this monstrosity, and then I'll have my regular."

"Oh no, you don't! Your fun sister will be the server tonight to ensure tons of enjoyment is happening all around!" She passionately looks at both Tansy and me.

I hold my hands up just as T does and says, "Okay, okay, fun all around."

It certainly doesn't take long for this place to fill up. We're two fish bowls deep into this birthday party, and Azalea places a third right in front of T. All that's left from our dinner and the brownies are a few small crumbs. I was thinking I would miss having cake, but honestly, Tansy's grin when I brought those brownies over with thirty candles more than made up for it. And somehow, with the fishbowls, the brownies worked. Hmmm, maybe it was the sea salt sprinkled on top.

Z thinks if we drink enough fishbowls, she'll get us up there to sing karaoke with her. I'm not convinced.

My attention is drawn to the stage as Tucker sings. I am always surprised at how well he carries a tune. For such a large man, his voice is mellow. He chose 'Check Yes or No,' and the whole place sings along with him.

I swear there are moments when I think he is looking directly at Tansy. It's so weird. Maybe there's someone behind us he is looking at?

The song fades out; Tucker still has the microphone in his hand.

"Hey everybody, thanks so much for singing along! Now, if we could, let's get the birthday girl on the stage! Tansy, come on up so we can sing 'Happy Birthday' to you!"

My sister narrows her eyes but grabs Azalea and me by

the hands to head up to the stage. "If I have to go up there, so do y'all," she grumbles under her breath.

Tucker leads everyone in the loudest version of 'Happy Birthday' I have ever heard, ending with cha-cha-cha! He passes the microphone to Tansy, and the next thing I know, Z and I each hold one too as 'Girls' Just Want To Have Fun' starts playing.

We didn't have any intention of participating in karaoke, but we sing like the rock stars we think we are. Tansy laughs and belts out 'want' as it drags on in the chorus.

As we walk back to the table, it seems Tucker has become the emcee for the night. "Great job, ladies! I think everyone here is having fun celebrating with y'all. Now, the night would not be complete if we didn't have Erika come up here and sing 'Dirt Road Anthem'."

As the music continues in the background, more drinks appear at our table. T leans over to Azalea. "Please be careful, remember that one time?" They both look over at me, concerned.

"Hey now, I'm fine. No, seriously. I am *so* good. Here, give me another one so I can show-ow you," I hiccup. Tansy and Z roll their eyes and laugh. "Plus, I mean, it's not like I would mind finding that duke again. Maybe if I focus real hard, I can go back to the same time and place," I joke.

Tansy raises her eyebrow at me, and Azalea's drink nearly comes out of her nose. Z may be the bad influence, but we all know how to let our hair down occasionally. "You did like that duke. How long was that trip?"

"Well, he was something. He had that sexy accent, and we had the most glorious picnic with deviled eggs and tiny sandwiches—and of course, strawberries and cream." I laugh. "But y'all both know I rarely stay more than one night in another time. I'd miss you both too much."

Goodness, the night has gotten away from me. "How late

is it?" I wonder aloud as Tucker is saying something I can't quite make out. Azalea grabs my arm and pulls me to the stage. "What are we singing?" We already did the only one I could think of.

"Oh, you just wait. You'll know this song." She is gleefully pulling Tansy by one hand and somewhat pushing me with the other. Once on stage, the first chords for 'Man! I Feel Like a Woman' resound, and the three of us immediately take our positions. We each face the right-hand side of the stage and perform just like we are in the music video.

By the end of the song, I am truly ready to sit where I stand. As I finally make my way back over to our table, another round waits for us. Z is still on stage and full-on performing 'Shake It Off'. I sit and grab a glass of water, dancing in my seat.

Every night we spend here is always a great time but tonight is a whole new level of hilarity. The drinks are flowing, and Tansy being carefree and happy—living in the moment—is precisely what I was hoping for.

Tucker gives props to Azalea for getting the whole place dancing, and then he follows up with, "Let's keep everybody moving with Gary! Come on up with your version of 'Welcome to the Jungle'. Everybody help him keep this party going!"

The entire bar sings along, and I glance at Rod to see if he's singing. He isn't, but he has a smile on his face. So, I think getting him to finally agree to karaoke nights is a win.

CHAPTER 2

HYACINTH

J'm not sure there is a word for how hungover I am. If I hadn't promised Rod I would help today, I would still be in bed right now. Maybe it won't be as wild as a typical Friday at Horney's. I can hope, right? Dragging myself across the room to my closet, I don't turn on a light until I absolutely have to. I should have known better than to say I would help the day after Tansy's birthday, but I didn't, and I won't let Rod down.

He has been the most consistent person in our lives since Mom's accident. Honestly, without his help, I don't know if Z and I would have been able to stay with Tansy. Up until the last five years or so, I didn't understand how impactful his presence had been during that time. Before the accident, he always watched over us. I thought it was in the way he watched over everyone in our town. I realize now he has always gone above and beyond the norm for us. So if there's a way that I can help him, I'll do it. Even though that means I need to get my shit together after being drunk last night.

After pulling my light brown hair up in a high ponytail with a few loose tendrils framing my face, I apply concealer and mascara to keep the makeup simple. I'm wearing my cute new linen frock dress that accentuates my curves, paired with low-heeled boots. Looking in the mirror one last time, I determine that this outfit will do. From my standpoint, it could definitely pass as a uniform for a pirate-themed bar. While Rod would never admit it, Horney's has those vibes.

Hornbuckle's Bar is a local institution. The story is, it was a tavern when actual pirates came through this little beach town. It even survived the Prohibition era by Rod's family turning it into a soda shop and ice cream parlor. Once prohibition ended, they reopened serving 'real drinks', as Rod likes to say.

Passing through the living room, Azalea is asleep on the couch. "Hey, Z, wake up!"

She throws a pillow at me. "Leave me alone," she grumbles. At least, I think that is what she said.

"I'm heading to the bar, but aren't you supposed to open The Garden this morning?"

"Nah."

Knowing it's impossible to wake her before she is ready, I quickly slip my sunglasses on because I won't survive the Florida sun without them. Turning back around, I grab a few more painkillers for the day.

I will make this work. If I say it enough times, it will eventually be true, right?

Stepping outside, I realize my car's not here. Events from last night, us staggering home, replay in my mind.

Oh, man! I left my car at the bar—guess I'm going on foot then. Moments like this make me thankful that I live in this small town. Everything here is within walking distance, which certainly makes my life easier, especially when you're too drunk to drive home. Maybe a little bit of walking and fresh air may help cure my hangover.

Rod looks up immediately as I step inside. "Wasn't so sure I'd see you this mornin'."

"I said I would be here, so here I am," I quickly retort.

He grins and walks with me to lock up my bag in the office. Now that I'm inside, it's dark enough that I can safely take off the sunglasses.

"It sure seemed like you girls had a good time last night," he says.

"Definitely! I was so happy to see Tansy let loose and have a good time. Do you know who took me home last night?" I inquire.

Rod blushes a little. "Well, actually, I drove you and Z back to your place. Tucker offered to take Tansy home."

Interesting. I will have to remember to ask Tansy about that later.

Luckily, the menu for lunch is as easy as it gets. And even if I didn't already know the options, there's an old, simple chalkboard sign with large letters:

'Lunch - The Burger, The Chicken, The Salad, No substitutions'.

I'm pretty sure I can handle that, even when I'm hungover. The lunch crowd is usually just a few locals who don't want to fix lunch for themselves.

This isn't exactly a tourist stop on the way to the beach. We don't even have a stoplight. The ocean is only a few blocks away, but it's mainly docks. It's several miles up the road to get to a beach. Most tourists stay in the town up there so they can be right by the beach. It works out for us. If we want to go to the beach, it isn't far. But we aren't tripping over tourists every day.

Tucker's voice carries from the kitchen making his

morning farm-to-table delivery, so I head that way to see if I can help. Really, I want to know about him taking Tansy home. When I walk through the swinging door, he looks shocked to see me upright.

"Wow, you look better than I feel."

"Yeah, well, fake it till ya make it. I'm barely hanging in there. What time did you make it home?"

He looks at his shoes.

What actually happened last night when he took my sister home?

He shyly responds, "It was pretty late, but I'm not complaining. Last night was fun." I raise my eyebrows, but he continues. "Being emcee was fun. I usually prefer to sit back and watch everyone else, but I had a good time doing it just for this one time."

Big Al, the cook, comes in with his order for Tucker's next delivery. "Tucker, these veggies look amazing," he praises, and I internally sigh.

That may be the most extended conversation I've ever had with him, but I don't think I can get more information out of him about last night. I guess I'll have to wait to talk to Tansy.

"Thank you, I'm real happy with how the crops are doin' this year," Tucker replies as he's heading for the back door.

I help Big Al put the vegetables away. Rod preps the main bar for the lunch rush.

Looking at the clock, I have one hour before I can take more of the pain caps that Z makes. Powering through, I head back out to the floor, the cacophony of voices filling the bar as people come in.

I slow down. There's something in the air, almost a presence I feel. Someone I don't recognize is sitting at the bar, but Rod has him covered.

Who is that? How do I feel he's here?

I have never felt someone's presence like this before. He's turned so I can't see his face. Damn it. His leather jacket hangs on the back of his chair, and I trace the lines of his muscled forearms. He makes that gray t-shirt look like it was tailor-made for him.

A local couple sits at a table, and I head over to get their order. With every step toward them, I feel like I'm getting weaker.

What is going on? I was feeling okay-ish when I left home. I am definitely feeling worse than I was an hour ago. How does that even make sense?

"Hey, y'all. I hope you're havin' a great day. Can I get y'all a drink, or are you ready to order?" See, I can do this, even with the room starting to spin. *I repeat what I think is their order.* "So you want a burger and a salad and two Cokes?"

"No, Hyacinth. We want the chicken and the salad and two Sprites."

Oops.

"I am so sorry, y'all. I'll be back quick as I can with your drinks."

When I get back to the kitchen, I'm taking more medicine. I'm sure if I get some Gatorade and one of the pain pills, I'll be okay again.

Al looks at me sideways. "You good?"

"Yeah, I'll be okay. Just got to get some more fluids in me, I think."

Taking the couple their sodas, the world tilts. I almost spill the sodas as I nearly miss their table. Something is going on.

The stranger's voice drifts across the room. Why does it feel like I should know his voice? I know everyone around here, so he's definitely not local. I can't quite place his accent as he's ordering the burger. There's no way I could know him. As I walk toward the back, I overhear him ask, "Who's the wench?"

What? Is he talking about me?

How could it even be possible the voice of a person I have never met would affect me like this?

It's not. It has to be the hangover. I step out back to get some fresh air; maybe I got too hot while I was in the kitchen.

Al hollers the food is ready, and I go back in to take care of the order. I'm counting the steps, trying to stay focused enough to make it back to their table. After leaving the couple their food, I go to sit down in the storage room. It's the coolest room in the place since that's where they stored the ice cream when it was a parlor.

As I pass by the end of the bar, I make eye contact with Rod. "I'm going to the back."

Grasping chairs and then the wall, I make my way to the storage room. I sit and count, trying to control my breathing.

In two, three, four; hold two, three, four; out two, three, four. It isn't helping.

I know I'm losing control, but there's nothing I can do to stop it. Rod's blurry figure rounds the corner just as he dissolves into darkness.

CHAPTER 3

LIAM

*H*ow is it that these two coasts, located on the same peninsula, look nothing alike? I traveled down to the Keys on the Gulf side. The water is so much calmer, and the sunsets were amazing, but man, I can't get over the sunrises on the Atlantic. Crossing what was called Alligator Alley on my bike, I'm just glad I didn't have to stop. I think this is what they talk about when they say people can disappear in Florida.

I took my time going down to the Keys and spent a few weeks there. It's easy to understand why people move there and don't leave, but I haven't found the one place that calls to me yet. Heading back up the Atlantic coast, most of these touristy little beach towns all look the same.

The sunrise drives are what poems should be written about. I've been sleeping better on nights when I could listen to the surf crash. I'm not sure if I want to travel somewhere where there isn't water again. Who would have ever thought

I would feel this way about the ocean? After my time in the Navy, I thought I'd had enough of it.

Not much in this life scares me, but lately, there is something about the ocean—its expansiveness. There are complete shipwrecks that have never been found centuries later, devoured by the sea. It never bothered me before, but for the past few weeks I've been dreaming of falling into the ocean.

Being along the coast, where I can hear it, but still be on dry land, is somehow soothing to my soul. It feels as if the sea is pulling me to stay near.

I'm planning one or two more days in Florida before heading further up the Atlantic Coast. It's pretty much wherever the wind takes me until I find where I'm supposed to settle. I don't know what I'm searching for, but there has to be somebody or something out there waiting for me, and I'll roam until I find it.

The main street in this little town doesn't even have a red light. Right down from this stop sign, the police station and fire station share a parking lot. Small towns don't get much smaller than this. I notice a bar sign coming up in a block or so. There are a few cars out front; maybe they're open for lunch. As I pull up closer, there is an anchor propped just outside the door that has an open sign. Looks like this will be lunch.

Crossing over the threshold, my eyes adjust from the brightness of the sun to the large bar down the width of the room, sections of high tops, and larger booths along the back wall. It looks like there may be a small makeshift stage in the far-right corner. I nod to the bartender as I head to the bathroom to clean up before sitting down.

It is very clear that this place has been here a long time, and the owner doesn't seem to care about updating the look. I bet the décor was about the same 130 years ago. I take my perch at the counter and notice the 'Lunch' chalkboard menu. Few choices, but that also means few opportunities for it not to be good.

"What'll be?" the barkeep asks in a deep, gruff voice. I guess being talkative isn't his strong suit.

"The Burger with a Coke."

He nods. This is the kind of service that works for me. Nothing makes me want to leave a place quicker than a bartender who doesn't know when to stop talking.

He pours my drink when the waitress goes past me to the couple that just came in. She is wearing a simple dress with her hair up. No one would call her a model, but she looks perfect to me. The dress hugs her curves perfectly. Any man who would prefer a Victoria's Secret model is missing out. This woman probably doesn't even know how beautiful she is.

As she saunters back to the kitchen to turn in their order, I glance at the bartender. "Who's the wench?" I'm assuming she dressed that way to go with what I can only assume is the pirate vibe of this place.

He glares at me with a look that could kill. "Stranger, that is no wench. You don't even need to be looking in her direction. She's too good for you," he replies through a clenched jaw.

With my hands raised in surrender, I lean back on my stool. "Whoa, man, I meant no disrespect. Honestly, I don't know if I have ever even used the word wench before. I'm sure you're right; she is too good for me, but isn't this a pirate-themed bar?"

I try to sound inquisitive and not judgmental. He cracks a smile at that. "That would be her and her sisters trying to make this place seem like it has 'character'. Name's Rod. My family's had this place for longer than this town's been here." He seems to have calmed down a bit.

I simply cannot take my eyes off her. She is more intoxicating to look at than any drink I have ever had. She takes the drinks over to the couple and nearly spills one of them. I don't know if she is nervous or what's causing her to be shaky. Rod seems to keep an eye on me and on her, too. Is he always this protective of her?

She hasn't looked up at me. There is something about this beautiful woman. I need to see her eyes.

My food comes out, and it is precisely what I hoped for —a perfect burger without the frills. You can tell the cook knows his way around the grill. The fries are fresh and seasoned perfectly. If everything is this good, I understand why the menu is as small as it is. I don't need more than that.

As I'm enjoying every bite, she walks by again, taking the couple their food. I'm focused on my burger and drink again as Rod makes his way toward her. She's stumbling a bit and looks like she needs to sit down.

It isn't two seconds later, Rod yells for someone to call 911. A big guy steps out and has his phone up to his ear already. I stop eating but stay out of the way. I don't think any of them would appreciate a stranger getting in the middle of whatever is happening back there.

The big guy tells Rod, "An ambulance is on the way."

I can barely hear Rod talking softly to the server. "Come on, Hy, wake up and look at me."

The first responders arrived so quickly; I wonder if they weren't already in their truck. I guess there's another benefit to a small town. Rod talks rapidly to them. He comes back in as they get her stretcher into the ambulance.

Rod looks at the cook. "I guess we're gonna hafta close down. I'm going to the hospital. At least 'til the girls can get there."

The cook looks frustrated but nods his head in understanding. Rod comes over to me and says, "Sorry, man, gonna have to close out the tab now."

I can tell he cares about what's happening more than just an employer caring for an employee. He's invested in her.

"Hey man, it's fine. Can't control emergencies. I know my way around a bar if you don't mind a stranger helping you keep it open while you're out." I know it'll be a stretch for him, but it's worth a shot to put some good karma out into the world.

He shakes his head no but then looks up at the big guy and seems to consider it. "I don't have time to show you around. If you need something, ask him."

Nodding to the cook as he walks out the front door he shouts, "Keep an eye on him."

CHAPTER 4

HYACINTH

*W*ow, my head really hurts. I must have hit it when I passed out. I pull my ponytail out to relieve the pressure. My head usually only hurts like this when I—wait.

Where am I? It's crazy dark in here. I thought I was in the storage room. I am in the back room? What?

"Breathe…just breathe. Stop and think. Don't panic. Figure out where you are so you can figure out when you are. Just give yourself a few minutes." And now I'm talking to myself. Great. Just Great.

Looking around, this is definitely the back room of Horney's. It's just cold, dark, and smelly. Did I travel back in time but stay here? I have never done that before. It's always going to a different location, usually a different country. This doesn't make any kind of sense.

Footsteps echo in the darkness, and I crouch behind a big barrel.

Oh, that smell—rum and who knows what else back here. I cover my nose.

"Finish yer cups, lads, but keep sharp. We've still a job t' do."

The voice gets closer, and then my hiding place is gone. I'm looking up at...the guy who was sitting at the bar? What? How? I don't understand!

"Whoa there, lass," he says in the familiar deep, rich voice.

Even though I am not short, he is easily a head taller than I am. I could wear heels, and he would still be taller than me. He has deep green eyes that crinkle at the edges, probably from staring at the sun reflecting off the ocean. His brown hair is long and tied back with what looks to be a short piece of leather. He has a long beard with hints of red in it. It's slightly unkempt, but that adds to his rugged look.

He leers at me and quietly says, "Can't say I've seen any lasses workin' here. Not 'less they be in service to Scarlet. So... is that why yer dressed like bait, then?"

I thought I was past the woozy-drunk feeling. But it comes back suddenly, and it's overwhelming as I sway. He grabs my waist to stabilize me, and our eyes lock.

As he slowly loosens his grip on me, neither of us can break the trance. We keep looking at each other.

Slowly and quietly, he says, "Ye've got a pull, like the sea herself. I can't stop starin'."

Shaking my head, I realize this is certainly not the man from the bar, but he is definitely my man. I need to figure out how I traveled back to—when am I, anyway?

How could I have possibly just traveled back in time, but stayed here? What am I supposed to do since I just found him?

Just beyond the wall, there is drunken singing. Suddenly, there's shouting, followed by a loud thud, then laughter. If there was any doubt about still being at Horney's, it is gone now.

"I need to get out of here," I whisper to myself.

He responds just as quietly, "Och lass, ye don't be leavin' without me…and not dressed like that. Unless ye mean to start a mutiny, 'cause every eye'll be on ye."

He pulls me close and out the back door of the bar. "I'll be the only one takin' what's mine."

He moves slowly and carefully, making sure I stay in the shadows of the building.

It was lunchtime when I traveled back, so it should be mid-afternoon now. That would explain why the shadows are only close to the building. Stopping, he leans his head toward a barrel. "Behind that barrel, quick. No sound, quiet your breath, and keep yer bloody head down."

Sheesh. He is bossy.

I peek out at the sound of muffled voices. He is directing a group of men carrying crates. Their clothes are more than slightly worn, almost to the point of tattered. Some of them had cut off their pants just below the knee, and others had patches on them. No one else seemed to be on the street right now.

I bet that's on purpose, but I wonder where the people are.

"By the devil's teeth, don't forget the rum!" the stranger says as he walks away from them.

He rounds the corner and then gathers me up close to him. "Best we get ye in somethin' less likely to cause a riot."

"Where is everyone?" I wonder aloud. With a smirk, "Chasin' after a few loose cows near the edge of town."

He puts his jacket around me as we step out of the shadows. This town is surreal. It doesn't look much different from my time. We have a few more buildings, but basically, not much has changed. I guess my little one-stop sign town just used to be a one-horse town instead.

Down the way is a building that has a door with bars across the window opening. I bet that's the jail, and there's a horse tied out front. There are a few horses and buggies about, but 'a bunch of horses town' doesn't quite have the same ring to it.

There is a mercantile, market, or whatever it's called down the road. I'm sure that's where he's taking me. Do they even sell clothes there?

He pulls me back into the shadows just outside a large house. He runs his hand through his hair and takes a deep breath. His eyes are focused on the back door of this building, so I search for the reason we're waiting.

"A brothel? You are *not* taking me to a brothel! I am not going in here." I move away from him.

He hauls me in, firm and fast, until I'm pressed tight to his chest. "Won't be but a blink. Scarlet'll fix ye up. I don't need every scab in this port starin' at what's mine."

What exactly does he mean his? I know what he means to me, but I don't know what he's thinking and now he's taking me in a brothel. Just what is he expecting to happen here?

The door swings open as if the woman knew he was near. He still has me glued to his side as we walk in. Each woman's eyes bounce between him and me. Do they know him? Does he frequent here? I know they're all wondering what in the world I am doing here with him.

A tall brunette, dressed in only a thin slip dress that hides nothing, steps forward and reaches toward me. "What's this then? Brought me somethin' sweet to play with, have ye?"

He knocks her hand away. "Enough, ye lazy tart. Get us to Scarlet, or ye'll regret it."

She pulls back. "Aye, fine, ye stubborn ol' seadog. Girls, be Scarlet busy, or is she takin' a break?

A well-endowed woman, with gorgeous red hair and the tiniest waist I think I've ever seen, appears at the top of the stairs and glares down at the brunette. "Aye, ye know I always be available for Dick. Can't believe ye waited this long to fetch me. I'da been right there if ye weren't all too slow about it."

Well, he obviously comes here often enough. She's always available for Dick?

He pulls me through the women, and we climb the stairs to who I assume is Scarlet. She looks intently at him as we approach. Her expression doesn't break, even though I am sure she has tons of questions.

We follow her into a room, and she leans against the closed door. "What in the seven seas is this? Comin' in here with a half-dressed woman, no less! Ain't nobody else would dare be so disrespectful in me establishment. I'll have no such nonsense in me halls, ye hear me?"

He growls at her, "Damn it, woman! I'm sorry, but weren't no other choice! Help me get 'er decent, will ye? We got to get to the Cinth 'fore the crew!"

Scarlet is stunning. Her red hair is curly and pinned up to fall perfectly around her heart shaped face. Light make-up accentuates her blue eyes, but her lips are painted a deep red. Her dress matches her eyes and pulls in at her tiny waist to create a perfect hourglass of her figure.

Her face didn't hide the surprise and disdain this time. "Are ye serious? Ye plan on takin' her on…. The crew's gonna have a bloody fit, and I'm not sure ye'll live to see it!" Her face softens the smallest amount. "Come here, lass, let me have a proper look at ye. Can't fix what I can't see, can I?"

For the first time, he releases his hold around my waist. I walk toward Scarlet. I don't speak; I'm too afraid it will be obvious I don't belong here. She walks around me and then picks up a gorgeous, deep-red skirt and a corset-looking garment.

"Lean this way, so I can get this skirt on ye. Can't be

wastin' time now, can we?" She winks at Dick as she talks to me. "Try to blend in, doll, but especially don't go lettin' anyone see ye without the overskirt. Ye'll be the talk of the town if ye do."

She pulls the bodice tight over my dress from this morning, but it hits the underwire of my bra. Giving me a funny look, she turns me around and helps me take it off. Then she cinches the bodice so tight I can barely breathe. When I turn back around, Dick's eyes nearly pop out of his head since my very ample breasts are much more prominent now.

I glance in the mirror, and my hand flies up to my chest. "My necklace!" I whisper as tears fill my eyes.

CHAPTER 5

TANSY

"Hey, Z, Rod's calling me. Can you cover the front?" I answer and put the phone to my ear.

"Tansy, Hy passed out in the back room."

"She's probably doing her time travel thing, Rod. Can you move her to the office?"

"Tansy, she wasn't acting right. She was wobbling and unsteady. When she goes on her trips, she's fine before she goes. This ain't right. I called the ambulance and I'm gonna follow to the hospital."

"Ok, we'll meet you there and call Dr. Harley!"

"Z, put the closed sign up. Rod's following Hy to the hospital, and we need to meet them there. Something about her passing out and it didn't seem like her normal time-travel stuff."

"What? She was fine this morning!" Z is already moving to the door to lock it and flip the sign around.

"I'll drive, and you call Dr. Harley from the car," I say, rushing for the door.

Z already has the doctor on the phone as I back out of the parking lot. *What did he mean she was unsteady? I know she had more to drink last night than she usually does, but even then, she has done this for so long now. She knows to go lie down. Why wouldn't she have recognized it if it's time travel like normal?*

"Okay, Dr. Harley is going to meet us there. He was already in town."

"Thank heavens, Hawthorne is still at Henry's parents' house. They aren't supposed to bring him home until tomorrow," I think out loud. Z nods in agreement, lost in thought.

Doc beat us to the hospital and is waiting for us as we sprint inside. He quickly ushers us to a quiet waiting room while filling us in. "Hi, girls. I have to agree with Rod, this doesn't seem typical of Hy. I'm admitting her to run some tests and start her on an IV. Y'all can't go in with her until she's settled in a room."

He pulled some strings to keep her out of the ER and get her straight into a private room. That's easier to do without extra people in the way.

"Rod, did you close the bar?" Z asks.

"Nah. Believe it or not, I left Al in charge with a drifter to help him. I hope the drifter ain't up to no good, but Al can handle him."

We stare at Rod in shock.

LIAM

"Hey, um, Cook?" He looks up at me. "I know Rod took off pretty quickly. Is there anything specific I need to do while it's slow? The bar is wiped, glasses cleaned, keg changed, and the soda gun's good. Is there a prep-list somewhere?"

"Yeah, he's got bar duties written somewhere. Just worry

'bout gettin' through today," he says without looking up from slicing tomatoes.

I don't know what it is about this place, but I like it. It's not really a diner, but it's more than a bar. It seems to be a gathering place for the locals. The reason for my filling in here sucks, but I hear the ocean while I work, and it's an easy pace. I think I might have found a place to stick around, at least for a little while.

CHAPTER 6

HYACINTH

As we walk back down the stairs, the girls openly stare. The brunette calls out, "See you soon, Dick!" He glares at her, and we keep walking out the back.

He still has me pulled close. "Dick—is that your name? I have to go back to the tavern. My necklace—I have to find it."

My voice is barely above a whisper, not wanting to draw attention. But I am not going anywhere without my necklace.

He slows and looks down at me. "It be more of a nickname, lass. We'll be makin' a quick stop at th' tavern, but don't go gettin' lost chasin' shiny trinkets. We ain't got all tide, y'hear?"

We pause at the back door of the bar, and he slowly creaks it open to make sure the room is empty. I look around trying to remember exactly where I was when I woke up. There are fewer barrels here now than there were earlier, so it should be easier to see, but I don't see it anywhere. It smells horrible in here, but I don't care. At least there aren't puddles all over. I fall down to my hands and knees to crawl around and feel behind the boxes in case it somehow slid behind them. Dick keeps looking out the door to make sure no one is coming, but he moves some of the boxes out of my way.

After a few minutes, Dick clears his throat, and my heart knows what he is going to say, but I'm not ready to hear it.

"We can't be lingerin' here any longer, we've got to get to the boat 'fore the crew beats us there."

"You don't understand. I need my necklace. I—"

His firm grip on my forearms halts my search. "We dinna have time, lass."

Tears well in my eyes, and I try to blink them back. I might know where I am. I don't know when I am. Standing in front of me is a man who is a stranger, yet I know him. And the urgency in his tone is enough to stop my search.

He pulls me close, and we walk toward the pier. Silent tears roll down my cheeks, but he keeps me walking with his arm wrapped around me.

As we board the ship, I struggle to stay steady. I've never been on a boat, even living on the coast. The wood is beautiful, but slick. Dick keeps his arm around me to help me move quickly across the deck.

I slowly realize it's a pirate ship. There are barrels I am certain were in the bar's backroom on this boat. *What have I gotten myself into here?*

We walk behind a set of stairs and into a room with several windows that overlook the back of the boat. With one hand, he locks the door behind us, and with the other, he circles my waist again. "Where is everyone?" I ask.

"Tyin' up loose ends. Best the townsfolk don't know what we were about 'til we've gone."

All I can think about is that I lost the last gift I got from my mom. She gave each of us girls a matching necklace the last Christmas before we lost her. It feels like I've lost her all over again.

He gently wipes the tears from my cheeks. "Lass, I can get ye a new trinket an' more besides. Don' fret so."

Dick pulls me toward the center of the room and slowly leans down to kiss my cheeks. I'm instantly pulled out of the turmoil in my brain, just by the gentleness of those kisses. *I just met him, but it feels like he's part of me already. Is this how the FateBond is supposed to feel?* His dark eyes stare into my soul. As his gaze drops to my chest, I didn't think his eyes could get any darker, but they do.

I have never had a man look at me like he does. Men look at Azalea like she's the prize, but not me. It's never been me. He lowers his head, and in the same movement, his hand is in my hair, and then his mouth is on mine. The hunger increases with each second the kiss continues. The moment we break away, I am immediately aware I have never been kissed like this before. Not just the hunger in it, but the passion, the connection I wasn't even sure I would ever experience. *Every touch just makes me want him more. I had no idea the FateBond would pull so strongly.*

We both try to catch our breath. He walks me over to the desk on the far side of the room and sits me in the wooden chair. This room is larger than I would have thought, but all I see is him silhouetted against the sun setting through the windows at the back. He is large and powerful, and though he's been gentle with me, I know there is an edge of violence there as well.

He immediately starts pacing and mumbling. When he finally stops, he turns to look at me, and slowly, deliberately, walks toward me. He stops right in front of me and kneels, taking my hands in his.

"If ye so much as touch that door or make a sound, it'll all be over. I swear, I'd do whate'er it takes to keep ye safe, even if it tears me apart. The only chance we've got is if ye stay hidden. If they've even a whiff ye're here, they'll turn on me, and ye'll never make it off this ship. Nod yer head. Show me ye understand. Ye can't leave this room. Not now. They're comin' aboard any moment, and if they see ye, it's done. I'll find a way. I promise ye that. We can't stay 'ere, they know me well. Once we reach the next port, we'll disappear. But for now, please. Ye've got t' stay quiet. Stay safe. Stay in here."

I slowly nod, "But, why?" I whisper. "Why are you doing all this?"

"Somethin' in me knows ye'. Deep as the tide runs true." He stands, turns and then walks out the door. The lock latches and the sound of heavy-booted footsteps grows further away.

I collapse onto the cot in the room. I lost Mama's necklace. The last thing she gave me, and it's gone. Tears continue to pour down my cheeks. I have found the other half of my soul, and he's a pirate! Mama's necklace is gone and to go home without *him* would be impossible.

I lost…her necklace.

I'm still on the cot when he returns a short time later with a bottle of rum. "Here ye go, m'lass. Just a wee bit t' steady yer nerves."

Hmmm, I wonder if that's some of the stolen rum? Lying on the cot, I try to get some rest. I wake a little later to a gentle touch. It's dark out, but I have no idea how late or how early it is.

"Hush now, lass. Yer safe. Quiet now and let sleep take ye."

His deep voice soothes me, and I drift away with his promise.

CHAPTER 7

TANSY

"*R*od, you can head back to the bar if you need to. I know Friday nights can get crazy. We'll keep you updated once…"

Dr. Harley comes around the corner, and we all stand up to meet him.

"Okay, girls. We have her settled in a room. You'll be able to sit with her in just a bit. I ran various tests to ensure this isn't a physical issue. To me, it looks like one of her trips. If that's the case, she'll wake up by tomorrow night as usual. You know she rarely stays away more than one night."

Z says, "One of us will be here with her until she wakes up. You know it will freak her out to wake up here instead of at home."

"I can stay this evening and spend the night. Hawthorne comes home tomorrow morning, though. I need to be there when he gets back home," I offer.

Rod nods. "I'm gonna head on back to the bar then. Don't

know how long the drifter was plannin' on stayin'. I'll come up early in the mornin' so you can go home to your boy. I can stay until Z can get here."

LIAM

Just as I finish wiping down the last of the tables, Rod comes back. He gives me a look and tips his head to the back. As I get to the kitchen, he tells the cook, "Doc has her settled. She's in a room but hasn't woken up yet. The girls are there, and I'll head up in the mornin' so Tansy can go home. They worked out a schedule."

He looks over at me. "How'd he do, Al?"

Al looks at me, shrugs, and grunts, "Fine."

Well, now, that was a ringing endorsement.

I follow Rod out of the kitchen to behind the bar as he starts to prep for the evening crowd. He stops to look around. Did I miss something? This place isn't large, and the lunch service wasn't exactly what I'd call a rush. I kept things cleaned and straightened all the alcohol, so we'll have easy access for making the drinks later. All the typical garnishes are prepped.

He crosses his arms and leans back against the counter. "You've done this before."

It wasn't a question. I give him a nod.

"Okay, then. You headin' out or wanna stick around for the evenin'?"

"I have nowhere to be."

After the Friday night crowd dwindles, Rod pours us each a beer and nods for me to sit with him at the corner of the bar. "You know your way around a bar, son." I nod once. "It looks like I'm gonna need some help around here for a bit. You want a job?"

"Sure. I like this little town so far." I usually take day jobs here and there to make ends meet while staying on the road. But so far, I wouldn't mind sticking around here for a while.

He nods once and asks, "Where are you plannin' to stay?"

"Well, I can sleep in my tent if there's not a motel nearby."

He gives me a long look before replying, "I have my old camper out back. Ain't nothin' special, but it's a roof over your head. You can stay there until you find a place."

"'Preciate it."

CHAPTER 8

HYACINTH

*T*he world rocks in an unsteady rhythm. I can't still be dreaming, and I definitely can't still be hungover. I slowly wake to a hand on my breast and a heavy weight around my middle. The rocking. This man. It all comes flooding back. He held me all night. My eyes are puffy and sore from crying, and he was a gentleman. Really? A pirate and a gentleman? I laugh, and it wakes him up.

"Mmmm. Nice way to wake, lassie."

"Ummm, Dick? I really need to use the ummm—relieve myself."

"Ah, lass, use the…errrr…head…errrr…pot…I'll grab us some grub."

I was so drained last night; I didn't even look around at all. It's a fairly large cabin, and more than big enough for several people. A chamber pot sits in the corner, so I quickly take care of that urgent need. I would love to brush my teeth, so I look around for something I can use. I know I won't find an actual toothbrush, but I'm hoping I can find something that will at least let me feel like I don't have morning breath when he comes back in.

The door creaks open, and Dick comes in with fresh bread, cheese, an apple, and an orange? From all the stories I heard about pirates, I honestly expected jerky and a moldy something.

"Lass, 'tis only our first day out. We got a bit o' bread and cheese. They won't last more'n a day or so. Ye best eat up while it's good, afore we are left with salt junk and hardtack."

"It's wonderful, thank you." After a pause, I ask him, "Yesterday, you said your name isn't Dick. Would you tell me your name?"

He laughs. It's a full, deep, throaty laugh that brings a smile to my face. He stands and bows gallantly. "Captain William Richard Doyle, at yer service, milady. Aye, the lasses do call me Cap'n Dick," he says with a roguish wink. "On account o' the size o' me sword."

Watered rum spews from my lips. "I will *not* be calling you 'Cap'n Dick'!" I sputtered. "I shall call you William."

With a grin, he replies, "Name me as ye please, lass. What'll I be callin' ye?"

"I'm Hyacinth. My sisters call me Hy," I replied tearfully.

As a tear falls down my cheek, he leans forward and gently catches it. The caress coming from such a rough man causes me to sigh. He gently touches my lips with his, then pulls back. "I'd have ye right here and now, me lass, but we've talkin' to do 'fore I go tend to the crew." He steps away, as if he knows that if he stays near me, we won't be talking. "How'd ye come to be hidin' away in the back o' the tavern?"

"That's a long story, William. How long do we have before you need to go?"

"Me first mate has th' deck handled a short spell, not fer

long. But I need t' know why 'tis you drag at me same as th' tide, same as th' sea herself? Have ye b'witched me, lass?"

"Hmmm…where to start? I'm not sure I can make it make sense. The pull you feel toward me, I feel it too. Do you believe in fate?"

"Believe in fate? Nay. I make me own fate. I set me course by will, not wishin'. I point this ship where I aim t' go, and I don't let wind nor wave decide for me. The sea might test me, but she don't rule me."

"Ok. I understand because I work for what I want too. But I allow the universe to help guide me. Kind of like how you use the stars to guide you. Fate guided me to you so we could find each other."

He looks at me a bit puzzled. "I've got to be topside fer a bit. I'll return and we'll speak more then. Afore I go, I need just a wee little taste." He pulls me to him for a sweet, gentle kiss. When I blink up at him, he swears and drags me hard against him, plundering my mouth for what feels like ages. He stares at my chest as I try to suck air into my oxygen-deprived lungs, and curses, "God's teeth. I'll be back. Don't leave this room or e'en crack the door."

CHAPTER 9

LIAM

*A*round mid-morning, a truck parks in Hornbuckle's parking lot, so I head on over to the bar. I guess it's more of a diner during the day. Rod goes in the back door, so I follow him in.

"How's your daughter doing this morning?" I ask as we reach the door at the same time.

"What?" He's definitely distracted. "Oh, she's not my girl. Her younger sister is there with her now. No change yet." As he turns toward his office, he mumbles, "She oughtta been, though."

Standing in the doorway, I ask, "What can I get started on?"

"We need to check out the back room and make sure everything's in order since that's where…" he trails off.

"Look, man, I'll take care of the back room. You need anything, yell for me."

Nothing looks out-of-place back here. It's definitely a

storage room, but it's cooler than I would have expected. It's almost like déjà vu. Looking around, I try to find out why this room feels so familiar, but I have no idea. I haven't been to the East Coast of Florida before, not even for the Navy. How is it so much cooler than the rest of the building? I'm not an engineer or anything, but I'm sure it has something to do with what the walls are made of. They are pale and uneven, made from a grainy stone. Up close, there are bits of sand and shell embedded almost as if they are fossils. It's cool and slightly damp when I touch it. I wonder what this could be made of?

It doesn't take long to get the cases of booze organized. Rod keeps things pretty straight. I noticed he's low on some of the beer we sold a lot of last night. I'll have to make sure he knows to order more. As I'm moving a case of beer, something glints on the floor. I pick up the slender gold chain, and it's warm in my hand, almost as if it shocked me. It's beautiful and dainty, with the letter H swirled in a heart. I put it in my pocket so I can give it to Rod later.

I head past the kitchen to make sure Al doesn't need help before I go out front. That cranky man informed me that no one messes around in his kitchen. A big, burly guy comes in with a crate of vegetables, so I turn to go up front. I stop when he asks Al if there's been any update on Hyacinth. I want to know how she's doing, so I listen.

"Rod said there wasn't any change this morning. I'm gonna make some lunch for him to take up to Z after the rush is over."

"What about Tansy? Isn't she up there with them?" the other man asks.

I don't hear Al's reply since people are coming in for lunch. I get up front just as a group of customers all get seated at a table. Nodding at Rod for him to stay behind the bar, I take orders. At this point, I am happy the menu here is simple.

Lunch was busier today than yesterday. Rod asked if I was okay to work this evening after already working the lunch crowd. Then he left to take lunch to whoever stayed up at the hospital.

This place is busier than I had expected, but it's nothing I can't handle for a while on my own while he's gone. The big guy from earlier comes in and has a seat at the end of the bar. "I'm Tucker. I supply the vegetables for Rod."

"Liam. Nice to meet you."

"Haven't seen you around here until today. When did you start working for Rod?"

"I was here yesterday when Hyacinth? I think her name is? When she fainted. I've worked in bars before, so I offered to stay and help."

Tucker's jaw dropped. "Rod just let you stay? That's incredible!"

I nodded. "I was surprised, honestly. But Al was here to keep an eye on me." I tell him in a mock whisper, "He still is."

Tucker laughs as I turn to assist another customer. "See you around, man."

CHAPTER 10

HYACINTH

*O*nce William leaves, I explore the room a bit. It feels like this is the entire end of the ship! The bed we slept on is large enough to fit his tall frame, but it's tucked into a little alcove, so it's more difficult to fall out in stormy seas. It looks as if there was once a curtain to close it off completely. Next to the bed are shelves. Almost as if there were a door there, it would be like a closet.

There is a huge table that would easily seat eight to ten, centered in the room with a map of some sort carved into it. I can't tell what it is, but I wonder if that's a star chart drawn on it?

One wall looks like it could be a bookshelf, with a desk in front of it. There are old tools, like I would expect to see in a museum, on it. A gorgeous brown globe, compass, sextant—I think that's what that thing is called—and a telescope. Why on earth would he need an hourglass? There is a book held open with a...dagger? What?

What kind of books would a pirate even want? These are gorgeous, leather-bound books. Maybe journals? His handwriting is lovely! And difficult to read. But so pretty! This isn't a journal; it looks like a ledger. It has where they've been and where they plan to go. *I wonder if it's true. I mean, if he writes where he's going, wouldn't he get caught? What else does he steal besides rum? That's all I saw them steal in town.*

Tucked behind the open book is a parchment-looking paper. It's a sketch made with a dark pencil. It might be charcoal. There are several of them. I think maybe they are sketches of places he's been. The one on top looks like it might even be Kingsdale. He's outstanding! There's one of a coastline, an island, and I think my favorite might be the ship.

OHHHH, there's a chest! I bet he has his pirate booty in there! Abandoning his desk, I crouch by the wooden chest to inspect it. It's bolted down, I guess to keep it from shifting in rough seas. The wood is dark with iron bands curving over the top, riveted tightly. The front corners have these elaborate carvings—on the left is a compass rose with stars, and on the right is a horrendous sea monster. Running my fingers over the grooves, the surface is smooth. This is beautiful. I'm not touching that lock – it's a coiled snake with an open mouth.

Azalea would love this chest, not because of the nautical stuff, but the history of it. I wish she could see it. Hawthorne would think it's cool to have a snake for a lock, and Tansy would have to get him one of those plastic ones to pretend to be afraid of. They should be expecting me home now. I don't know if there is a way for me to let them know I'm ok. Maybe I can find a way once we are on land again.

The door to William's quarters rattles like someone is

trying to open it. I start to call out but then remember William saying I couldn't even crack it. He must have locked it. *Did he lock me in here?*

"Oi, Cap'n! Why's yer door bolted tight? I was gonna empty the blasted head!" someone shouts outside, and he did not sound pleasant at all.

"Hands off me cabin, ye nosy bilge rat! I can see to me own business, including the head!" William shouted back.

"Aye or ye just don't want us seein' what's in there. Secrets don't dump as easy as bilge." That sounded like a third pirate.

William's voice comes closer, and a quiet threat laces his tone. "I don't repeat meself, mate. Last soul who didn't listen's still afloatin' in pieces."

His voice is deadly. I would not want to be the person he's speaking to right now.

William opened the door and immediately locked it. He wrapped me in his arms, breathing heavy. "Why does it matter if you dump the chamber pot?" I ask quietly.

"I'm the Cap'n, not the cabin boy. Scrubbin' is for swabs." I don't understand. He looks at me and sighs. "No wenches on the ship. They be a curse upon the sea. Storms follow 'em and mutiny's ne'er far behind. They can't be knowin' I brought ye aboard, lass."

I glare at him. "So I'm causing a lot of trouble for you already."

"Trouble, ye say? Bah! A handful o' days, no more'n a week, and we'll vanish like mist off the water at dawn. So, I ask ye, can ye keep yer head down, stay in the cabin, and no' let them know ye're even aboard?"

I can't even pretend not to be afraid. Shaking, I tell him, "I will try."

"Tryin' won't do, lass. If ye fail, we'll be feedin' the fishes."

A shiver runs down my spine at his admission. He willingly brought me with him, despite not understanding our connection, and risking his life to keep me by his side. Seeing my fear, he pulls me close against him. I wrinkle my nose, and he laughs. He smells like 'the fishes' already! I'm sure I don't smell much better.

He leans in to kiss me quickly. Just as in the times before, he stops and stares. I am not a small woman, but he seems to really appreciate the size of my breasts with this corset pushing them up to my chin. He gently drags his finger across the top and softly groans. It feels like he is almost in a trance as he lightly traces the edge of my top. As he slides a finger just under the edge, I gasp. He startles out of his trance and leans in to kiss me again.

"I could linger 'ere all day admirin' these beauties, but duty's callin'. I'll be back soon, lass."

He kisses me quickly, then grabs the chamber pot and disappears out the door. The lock clicks into place and his footsteps fade away.

I don't know how long I sat staring at everything on his desk and thinking about what brought me here. I feel the FateBond in place. Every time he touches me, it brings our souls closer together. Can I even feel that? I know that though I shouldn't, I trust him completely. *A pirate.* I trust a pirate completely. I'm still sitting at the desk when I hear the key in the lock again. Time is passing so oddly today. It's getting dark as if the sun is already setting.

CHAPTER 11

AZALEA

*S*itting in Hy's room, with the heart monitor beeps my only company, I send a text to Tansy, letting her know Rod came by.

> Me: Rod stopped by with some lunch for me so I wouldn't have to leave.

Thankful for the distraction, I inhale the deliciousness that is Big Al's chicken tenders. Today is one of those days that I'm glad Rod always chooses for me. I slept last night confident that Hy would wake up today, but now I'm not so sure. It doesn't feel the same.

> T: What did he bring?

> Me: Fried chicken salad with jalapeno ranch.

Taking a hearty bite, I moan as the flavors burst in my

mouth. No one's ranch is as good as Al's. My phone chimes with another message from Tansy.

> T: Yum. I just had a PB&J. I'm gonna close at 3. Mae will watch Hawthorne for the afternoon so he and Hayden can have a playdate. I'll be up after I drop him off. Need anything?

I glance at the bottled water Rod brought and grin. He's always looking out for us and our hydration.

> Me: A sweet tea would be great.

> T: Gotcha, Sis.

I read her last text as a nurse comes in. They have been in and out checking Hy's vitals and such all day, but nothing has changed. If she hasn't woken up by the time Tansy closes the Garden, I'm thinking I'll offer to watch Hawthorne for her to stay up here again. He loves staying with me above the shop, anyway.

Today has been at least a little productive. I never stop when I'm at the shop, but being here, I've had time to research some more homeopathic recipes. I love looking through really old books with tinctures in them. Most of them aren't helpful. But digging through to find one good recipe is worth it. It always feels like I'm on a treasure hunt.

I'm reading about the benefits of willow bark when Doc comes in to check on Hy. I quickly mark my page as he closes the door and sits.

"Z, I'm not feeling so good about this. She's normally at least starting to fidget and stir by now. She's basically acting as if she's in a coma. There's a new supervising physician here, and I don't think I'm able to keep him off her case if she doesn't wake up today."

"But, Doc!," I whisper-shout. "He won't understand how special she is, and that she's not just a comatose patient! If he tries to pull her out, we don't know what will happen. I know I never asked about any of your other patients. Do you know anyone who can help us?"

Dr. Harley sighs and leans forward to take my hands. "Z, honey, I know there are other people like you girls. I'm fairly sure there are even some around here. But no one has ever come to me like your mama did. We were always afraid we could put a bad spotlight on you girls if I poked around asking questions."

"Doc, you know we love and appreciate all you've done for us. I guess stall the new doctor as long as you can. Hopefully, she'll wake up tonight. We know she rarely stays gone for more than one night. She should be back tonight and upset she caused all this trouble with some wild story to tell."

Doc pats my leg and sighs. "Okay, Z. Try not to stress out too much if you can help it. I'll stop by before I go home. Do you girls need anything?"

"Not that I can think of. Rod said he would bring dinner for us. I know Tansy will come up as soon as she closes The Garden. She set up a playdate for Hawthorne for this afternoon so we could both be here for a little while. We'll text you if we need you."

CHAPTER 12

HYACINTH

*W*illiam comes in with a cloth bundle in one hand and the chamber pot propped under his other arm. Ew! He sits the pot back in the corner and comes toward me at the desk. Taking the bundle, I find more bread, cheese, and oranges. He grins at me when my eyes light up at the oranges.

"Aye, lass, noticed ye likin' the orange earlier. Reckoned to bring ye another."

I thanked him for it and started in on the bread and cheese. "Are you done working on the deck today, or do you have to go back out?"

"The night's long yet, I reckon there's still some talkin' left t'do. Guess I'll be stayin' in tonight and tendin' to what's mine."

I had just put an orange slice in my mouth when he called me his again. "Is that what I am? Yours?"

"As sure as the sea be wet, ye belong t' me and make no doubt o' it. Go on then, tell me, lass. I need t' hear your tale."

While I eat my dinner, I tell him and hope he won't think that I'm crazy. I tell him I am basically from the town where he found me, just a few hundred years from now. I tell him how my sisters and I aren't 'witches', we have special talents. And that fate brought me to him because we have a Fate-Bond, and that's why we feel so strongly about each other so quickly. As I talk, he watches me. No reaction. Maybe that's why he's the captain? He keeps a great poker face. I honestly don't know what he's thinking.

"Please don't feed me to the fishes," I whisper softly—for the first time, afraid of him.

This scary man starts to laugh. I mean, he's a gorgeous, scary man. But still. He is *scary*.

"So ye just walk through time like I walk the deck? D'ye just vanish from one and hop to the other?"

"From what my sisters have said, I'm still there, but I'm asleep? I guess that's how to describe it? I faint and don't wake up until I'm back. It's usually just a day or so. Normally, I would look around the time I'm in for a bit, then focus on home and pop back to my time. I have never gone into the future, but I have gone back to different times and places quite a bit. This is the first time I haven't ended up in another place, just a different time. I think it was because I needed to find you."

"What magic binds us so? I feel it in me blood, draggin' me to you. Why, lass? What be this pull between us, like the tide to the moon?"

I tried to explain it to him as I remembered Mama talking about it. She didn't talk about it much. I just knew that it was supposed to exist, and now I know it does. "The FateBond links two hearts when the couple touches for the first time.

With each touch, it'll grow stronger. It can only happen if both people are willing to accept each other's heart and hold true to one another. Neither one will be complete without the other. Stronger than wedding vows. Once accepted, only death can break the bond. If a person isn't willing to hold true and faithful, the bond won't take hold."

"Why in blazes! What fool turns their back on a thing like that, eh?" He scoots my chair closer to him with his foot. "So, every time I lay hands on ye, this bind o' ours tightens, eh? Ye crave me more, don't ye, Wench?"

I whimper as he gently strokes the top of my breast again, pulling me in closer and sliding his hand inside the top to move the material out of his way. He places a soft kiss on each breast, then buries his face between them.

I giggle a bit, and he looks up at me with questioning eyes. "You're going to smother yourself."

"Aye." He winks. "If I'm goin' down, I'll go smilin'. Hell of a way t' meet the end." He immediately latches on to one nipple and cups the other breast in his hand.

"Oh!" I swear my ovaries explode.

I grab his head to hold him to me, loosening the tie and knocking it out of the way. When I scrape my nails through his hair, he releases my breasts with a groan and lifts me from the chair so he can untie the stays on my corset. It's incredible to see this man, with his hands shaking, dragging the strings loose. I pull his shirt loose from his pants. Good Lord, his muscles. I freeze to look at the beauty of this man as he pulls the shirt over his head, shaking his long hair loose. The smattering of hair across his chest, leading to, oh my, clearly defined muscles, tattoos, and a happy trail leading south. Wow. *This man is mine?*

He unties the overskirt that Scarlet gave me yesterday and helps me step out of it. I'm left in my dress that I love and thought was pirate-y.

"Tell me, lass. Is this meant t' be a dress? 'Tis soft enough t' sleep in. This be what women wear from your time? What do ye do dressed so? Ne'er ye mind. Ye can talk later, Wench."

CHAPTER 13

LIAM

*T*oby Keith's 'I Love This Bar' plays on the radio. I've been in a lot of small-town bars, and this place feels different. It's dinnertime, and the place is packed. Rod mans the bar itself while I handle the tables. It's not so big that I can't handle them on my own, but I am busy.

Feels like I've barely turned around, and the crowd is changing—less dinner and more bar patrons. Rod nods for me, so I head that way.

"Can you handle this on your own for a while?" I look at him as if he's nuts. *Sure, Rod, I can handle a Saturday night packed house for you, why not?*

"I'll be back as soon as I take the girls some dinner," he continues while packing up two burgers and fries.

"Sure," I say, because how can I tell him no?

He heads out with a satisfied nod, and I move behind the bar. I am definitely busy. The crowd doesn't seem to mind coming to the bar to order and grab their drinks to take back to their tables. I am in full shake mode when I notice Tucker grabbing food from the kitchen and taking it to a table. I give him a nod and go back to serving up drinks. He keeps up with the food, while I keep up with the booze. When he slows for a moment, he comes over to the bar.

"This is busy even for a Saturday night. I stopped in to see if Rod had an update on Hy, but Al told me he had just left to go up to the hospital. I figured I'd at least help out while he's gone."

"It wasn't this crazy when he left. The dinner crowd was slowing down. It's not always this busy on Saturdays?"

"Well, I usually deliver here on Thursday afternoons and then stick around to watch karaoke or hang out for ladies' night. Ever since the girls talked Rod into letting them do that, it's become a gathering place. It's a good time. The rest of the week, I deliver in the mornings."

Before Tucker could say much more, Rod was back. We both waited for him to say something, but he shook his head and went to the kitchen. I tipped my head to Tucker for him to follow Rod. Maybe he could find out what's up without all the people around.

I go back to pouring drinks while I wonder what could be wrong with the cute server from yesterday. I may not know her, but I can't stop thinking about her—and worrying about her.

CHAPTER 14

HYACINTH

*M*y jaw drops open at his 'wench' statement, and he grabs my face with both hands to plunder my mouth again. I swear I could kiss this man for all eternity, and it wouldn't feel like it would be enough. He slowly pulls the dress up and over my head. I'm incredibly thankful that I wore my favorite lace cheeky panties to the bar yesterday. Even so, I'm very aware that this man is seeing my body for the first time. He steps back and stares at me. I know I'm not small, but I have great curves, and I'm not ashamed of them. The longer he stares, I get concerned that maybe my curves aren't all that great.

"By the gods. 'Tis like ye were carved for my hands alone," he whispers reverently as he reaches for me again. I grab hold of the waist of his pants to hold on as he softly kisses along my jaw and down my shoulder. He backs slowly to the bed and sinks down onto the mattress, still kissing his way down my body. He alternates between my breasts, sucking one tight nipple into his mouth and pinching the other almost to the point of pain. Almost.

Fisting my hands in his hair, my legs buckle from the pleasure. I'm not entirely sure what to do. My few lovers were just flings and weren't that great. I enjoyed them, but I have never experienced this kind of pleasure. And he's only touching my breasts so far. Good grief, I'm going to come just from this!

As my legs give way, he lifts me to straddle his lap. His strong hands trace the lace pattern on my panties. "If ever there were a tool o' torment made just fer me, this be the one," he rumbles quietly just before he rips the lace to lightly trace the skin it had covered. I whimper, and he flips us around and over so that he is hovering over me. Leaning down, he kisses me quick and hard. William shifts himself to the side and quickly removes his pants. I swear my jaw drops open at the sheer size of him.

"That's not gonna fit." I stare with huge eyes.

His grin turns a bit wolfish when he looks at me and growls, "Ah, lass, it'll fit. The gods carved you soft and sweet and tight jus' fer me. Ye're meant to be filled by nothin' else."

He rolls toward me to latch onto a breast. He sucks and bites and soothes until I'm squirming. His fingers go back to tracing the lace that he ripped. He tugs what's left of the fabric so that I'm entirely bare for him. I fist the blanket as he kisses his way down my body. By the time he reaches his goal, I'm squirming in anticipation.

He licks up my center, and I buck up off the bed. "Keep that sweet mouth quiet now, lass. I've no mind t' share the sounds ye make." He slides up my body to cover my mouth in a deep kiss while keeping his hands busy playing with my pussy. He has two fingers buried deep, and I try to stay quiet, holding back the scream through the orgasm he triggers. Instead of slowing me down, he slips in another finger, and I groan at the fullness, bucking against his hand. "Please, William, I need you now."

He lines himself up and slowly slides in. He is enormous, and I'm still not sure he'll fit. I whimper a bit as he goes deeper.

"Relax, love, ye can take me." He shifts so that he can pinch my nipple again, and I gasp. He slides further in and pulls back, rocking in and out while he switches to the other breast to give it a bite, then soothe the pain away. I am so full of him, and I know he isn't even fully seated in me yet.

Curling down, he kisses my jaw and works his way back to nibble on my earlobe. He shifts more and bites down hard just above my collarbone as he slams all the way in. He freezes in place as I wrap my arms and legs around him to hold him in place.

"Ye alright, love?"

"So fucking full," I mumble into his neck. He backs away, looking at me as he shifts his hips ever so slightly. My whole body shivers as the pleasure from that small movement spirals through me. Now that he knows he isn't hurting me, he shifts, burying his face between my breasts while he languidly moves until I'm shaking again. He covers my mouth with his to swallow the scream I can't contain.

He increases his pace as sweat slides down his back. "One more, lass, jus' give me one more."

I shake my head from side to side as he pistons in and out of me, hitting places I didn't even know were possible. As my body tightens again, he buries his face in my neck and explodes in his orgasm that leaves us both shaky and gasping for breath.

He slowly pulls out of me and rolls us so he can hold me against his side. As we move, I must make a face because he gives me a long look. He pushes me onto my back and grabs the blanket to clean me up gently. I hiss as he wipes me, then moves me so that he can shift the top blanket out of the way.

I freeze, realizing what I just did and what we didn't do. "Oh! My! God! We didn't use protection!" Do they even have protection in this time? "Oh my God!"

"Easy now, lass. Protection? From what, the sea? The stars? I'm the fiercest thing you'll ever face, and I'd never raise a hand to you, me love. Ye don't need nothin' but me for protection. What is it that ye think I'd allow harm ye?"

"You big brute! I don't want to get pregnant!" I sob.

"Aye, what's done is done, and I can't take it back. I swear to the stars above, it won't happen again. Will that ease the ache in ye?"

"No!" I wail, "I still want sex!"

"Aye, there's my Wench," he smirks at me. "If it's peace ye want, I'll pull out. Though truth be told, there ain't a part of me that doesn't crave stayin'."

He soothes and snuggles me, deep in thought. We're both quiet, living in the moment of finding our FateBond. Who knew that a pirate would want to snuggle? I'm curled up next to him, propped on his impressive chest, tracing the compass rose tattoo there. "What does this mean?"

"'Tis stars to bring me safe passage and a compass rose, lass. Me soul w' ne'er be lost. I guess 'tis true. She led me you."

"What about the one on your arm? Is that a kraken and anchor—like on your treasure chest?"

"Ah, so ye' seen that, did ye now? Th' monster has the fury o' the sea, and the anchor bears the weight o' me duty. The anchor kept me steady when the world was nothing but storm and salt. But the Kraken, she's the part of me no one ever tamed. 'Til you. Never had the mind t' be tamed 'til you came along."

With a deep sigh, he says, "Alright now, lass. Tell me more 'bout the strange twist o' fate that brought ye here t' me."

"Well,. I grew up knowing my sisters and have gifts, but we didn't know anyone else like us. Mama had her flower shop, Meadow's Garden, and she could add a bit of extra life and beauty to the flowers and plants. Tansy, Azalea, and my gifts were different, though. We figured out what they were when we, well, when our hormones changed." I blush, but he never slows his rhythmic stroking of my body. My arm, my back, even down to my hip.

"We figured out Tansy's gift when she got upset, and a massive storm suddenly appeared from nowhere. As soon as she calmed down, it cleared up. Now that only happens when she is really emotional, and honestly, she tries to keep her emotions under tight control because of it." I pause for a moment before continuing.

"Azalea is absolutely stunning. She was beautiful even as a child. Everyone gravitates to her. She is honestly as sweet as she is lovely. She is wild and crazy and fun, but when she is helping someone, she settles. She empathizes with people so much that it's almost like she can take some of their pain, and she always tries. She is incredible at helping people feel better." I stop again. This is going to be hard for them, and I miss them already.

I shift so that I'm snuggled in tighter and not able to see him at all to tell him about me. He stops stroking me and pulls me in tight. "Go on, lass."

"The first time I stepped through time was terrifying. Some girls were being mean at school. I was crying and running home when I fainted outside Horney's. Rod came running out and picked me up to take me into his office. He called my mom and, of course, everyone was freaking out."

"I woke up in this beautiful garden outside a castle. I don't really know when or where it was. It was so peaceful, and gorgeous flowers were everywhere. I lay down in the shade to take a nap, and when I woke up again, I was back in Rod's office at the bar. That time, I was only gone a few minutes, and Mama hadn't even gotten to the bar before I came around." I smile a bit at the memory of Mama and Rod fussing about it.

"It was a while before it happened again, several months at least. Now I've been to lots of times and places. But I have never been able to control it. I only have a bit of control over when I go home. I used to think that if I went to sleep, I would magically go back to my time, but that didn't happen when I traveled to France. I thought I would certainly go home after falling asleep that evening, and I was excited to tell my sisters all about the fantastic sights I had seen. I didn't, though. By the third day, I was desperate to go home, so I took a nap. Finally, I went back. That was the only time I've been gone more than just one night, and it's when I learned that I have to sort of reach for it to be able to go back home."

I'm terrified he's going to think I'm crazy. Even with the insane attraction, he couldn't possibly believe me. He's been quiet for so long that I think he may have gone to sleep. I lift my head to look up at him, and he's just watching me. He leans forward a bit and softly kisses the top of my head.

"Alright now, that's enough outta ye fer now. Close yer eyes and get some rest, lass."

I stiffen and try to pull away from him. He rolls toward me and pulls me back.

"And where d'ye think yer slippin' off to, eh? Ye've given me a lot to ponder, and I've questions yet." He grabs my hair to pull my head back for easy access to my mouth. After a breath-stealing kiss, he says against my mouth, "But ye'll be needin' a bit o' rest, lass. I've still got more plans for ye."

CHAPTER 15

AZALEA

I don't understand why Hy isn't awake yet. When she first time traveled, there was one instance when she was gone for two nights. Mama got so upset. That's when she told Doc everything she knew about our powers. Hy hasn't been gone that long since then.

Mama would be disappointed to know I still don't have any powers—not actual powers. I love what I do with the tinctures and oils, and they help people. However, I am using the hard-earned knowledge I have from constantly studying. There's nothing magical about it.

There's a soft tap on the door, and T comes in, her face pinched with worry. "Hey, T. Everything go okay today?" I ask.

"I guess. It was just an odd day, on top of all this going on with Hy. I hope I didn't mix up any of the orders."

I look at Tansy. Really look at her. "What's wrong? Is

Hawthorne okay?" I think for a moment and demand, "Is Dr. Douche being an ass again!?!"

She smirks at me before she replies, "Hawthorne is fine. He and Hayden were planning some fort thing to build on their favorite game. Mae said to let him stay the night. Once Hawthorne heard she was making spaghetti for dinner, his only question was asking if she's making her special bread to go with it." She levels me with a direct look. "And you know Douche is always an ass, but I didn't even talk to him today."

"Okay," I say, drawing out the word. "Then what's wrong with you?"

She sighs and very softly says, "Tucker came by today. He brought me some of his lettuce, tomatoes, cucumbers..." Much firmer, she adds, "Does he think I need to lose weight or something? He brought me stuff to make a salad! I don't understand this at all!" She sniffles, and a tear rolls down her cheek.

"Whoa, wait just a damn minute here! Tucker brought you stuff from his garden? Why?"

"I don't know. I wish I did. He took me home from the bar on Thursday night. Honestly, I was so toasty I fell asleep in his truck. I don't even remember going inside the house. Ugh, can we please change the topic and talk about something else?"

Rod steps in the door, saying, "Change what topic, girls?" He hands the bag over to me, and I inhale deeply, smelling those amazing fries.

"Tansy was just saying that Tucker took her home Thursday night, and today he brought her some veggies from his garden. No big deal, right?" I catch him up as much as I'm comfortable saying. T is bright red and hiding behind her hair to unpack the dinner.

"Hm. Okay. Anything new?" Rod asks. He looks like he hasn't slept at all.

"Doc came in earlier and basically said all the tests he ran show nothing is wrong. There's a new supervising doctor guy, and Doc doesn't think he can keep him off the case if Hy doesn't wake up today. He said he would stop back by to check on us before he leaves for the night."

Rod goes over to touch Hy's hand and whispers something to her. He turns back to us and says, "Well, I left the drifter to cover while I brought you girls dinner. I'd better head back. Y'all call if y'need me, okay?"

Tansy stands and wraps him in a long hug and kisses his cheek. "We will call you immediately if anything changes or we need you. I promise."

TANSY

I look over to Azalea. "I don't understand why she hasn't come back. She usually stays away for only one night at most. There's only been one time she stayed away longer than one night. What could possibly be wrong?"

Z looks at me, her gaze full of worry. "I was just thinking about the same thing a little while ago. I talked to Doc about finding someone who knows more about the powers she has, but he said that Mama didn't want him to find help in case it brought us attention. I think Mama knew more than what she told us about it."

"I'm sure there are more people like us, but what would it cost us to find them? Mama told stories about the old family tales. I don't know what she was waiting for before telling us more, but then she was gone. I'm a little afraid to stir the hornet's nest if she was trying to protect us from something. We may not have a choice but to try to find some help." I think about what could happen if people found out about us all.

"Z, go get some rest. I know it's exhausting being here all

day. The shop is closed tomorrow. I'll stay here and we can switch off in the morning again."

Azalea looks over at me and agrees to go home. "Will you try to get some rest while you are here? That chair folds flat to make a bed. I know you won't sleep well, but at least rest. I'll see if I can find anything in my notes at home to maybe help bring her back."

We share a long hug before Z heads home. Left alone, I have nothing but the monitor's steady beeping and racing thoughts to keep me company. Rain starts up outside, and I know that I need to calm down. The last thing we need is for me to cause a flood, adding to our troubles.

CHAPTER 16

HYACINTH

*I*t was still dark outside, but the rising sun cast a little light over the ocean. I can honestly say I don't mind being woken up by William softly kissing my shoulder. "Mmmm, good morning," I say groggily.

"Good morn', Wench," he responds as he shifts us so that he is on top of me, with one breast in each hand, and buries his face. I giggle, and he lightly bites me, then immediately kisses the hurt away.

He takes his time kissing, nipping, sucking, all the while I'm squirming, trying to find the friction I want. As he pops off one nipple to look at me and grin, he slides his hand between my legs, and I groan. Not the good kind either. He freezes and looks up at me with a question in his eyes.

Completely embarrassed, I tell him, "I guess I'm a little sore from the three times you woke me last night."

"Ah, lass, I know just the thing t' cure ye." With a wicked smile, he slides down so his face is between my legs. With one slow lick, I come off the bed with a moan. Never in my life would I have expected this. His teeth, tongue, and beard combine to drive me insane. He slings one arm up to cover my mouth with his hand as I scream from the orgasm that crashes through me.

"Quiet now, Wench, else I'll have a mutiny on me hands." He works his way slowly back up my body until he stops at my mouth. Kissing me softly, he tells me to go back to sleep for a while.

He gets up and grabs his clothes, and I stutter at him, "But, what about you?"

He gives me his smirk and leans in for a quick kiss, and boob grab. "That was for you, love. I'll get me own later. Now, back t' sleep w' ye. I'll be bringing ye some rations later to break yer fast." He covers me with the blanket before leaving me alone in the room.

I have nothing to do but stay in this room, and since I am completely exhausted from last night, I decide to laze about in bed and try to get some rest.

CHAPTER 17

AZALEA

I am going to find something to help pull Hyacinth back. There has to be something I can do. I have some of Mama's old books in the tall cabinet at the Garden and I haven't even gone through everything in there yet.

Turning on some jazz, I get to work. It's loud enough to fill the quiet without taking my focus. It's the music that steadies me, calming my nerves and softening the chaos swirling around me. I take a deep, bolstering breath as I open the cabinet, and immediately I know I need to pull everything out and organize it into piles. A long time ago, I went through most of these books, but my organizational skills were not as good as they are now. I need to pull things out and put them into stacks according to what I can use.

Once I think everything is out, I organize. Something feels wrong. I stop and look around. I swear, a chill just went down my spine. Mama said never to ignore when you feel that slight whisper of other. I never knew what she meant by that until just now.

I go back over to the cabinet and feel along each of the shelves. Nothing. Whatever I'm supposed to find is in this cabinet. I grab the step stool to check the top shelves. Running my hands along the weathered wood, I tap and find a hollow sound at the back. What on earth?

I get down and text T.

> Me: Did you know there's a false back in Mama's cabinet on the top shelf?

Her response is almost immediate. So much for resting like she's supposed to be.

> T: What are you talking about?

Pacing the shop floor, I type as quickly as my fingers can.

> Me: I decided to look through Mama's old books to see if I could find something to help Hy. The top shelf only goes halfway.

> T: WTF? Can you open it?

I stare at the betraying cabinet. The chill down my spine is screaming. Part of me wants to run, but I can't let Hy down. The answers are here. I know it.

> Me: I'll let you know.

I diffuse some oils to help with focus and the anxiety that is almost overwhelming me. Hmmm. Bergamot, rosemary, and citrus should do the trick. I don't want anything to make me sleepy, so those should be perfect.

Grabbing the ladder and a portable light, I head back to

the cabinet. Once I set the lantern on the shelf, it shines on the seam of the false back up against the sides of the shelf, but I can't see any way to move it without breaking it. As I run my fingers along the edges, it feels as if the side and center are pressed against something, but the rest of it is loose. I would prefer not to break this if I don't have to. Pushing on the corner doesn't make it move. I wonder what else it could be? I look back over at the stacks I removed from the shelves to see if I can find any inspiration. There's a magnet in the shape of a group of tansies. Could it be a magnetic closure, maybe?

I run the magnet in front of the corner, and something clicks. Oh wow! That's cool! I release the other corner, then go to the center. Carefully moving the back out of the way, there's a row of old notebooks. I pull one out; it's an old composition book.

Unable to contain my excitement, I text T.

> Me: Mama kept journals. There are composition books and spiral-bound notebooks and some nicer journals.

T: 😊

I flip through the journals. Dust flies with each cascade of pages. My eyes burn at seeing Mama's handwriting.

> Me: There are letters.

T: What do you mean, letters?

I run my fingers over the thick embossed paper. My name, delicately scrawled across the parchment.

> Me: Envelopes. With our names on them. I'll bring them tomorrow.

These journals go back to when Mama was in high school! The last entry is from the week of her accident, so I grab that one and the letters. I don't want to go through these without Tansy and Hyacinth, and I'm exhausted. This feels like something I need my sisters for. I text Tansy to let her know.

> Me: I'm heading to bed.

> T: Okay, see you tomorrow. Or I guess later this morning.

> Me: Try to sleep.

CHAPTER 18

HYACINTH

The door opens again and as I slowly open my eyes; I am surprised to realize how bright it is outside. I must have slept for a long while.

William gives me his smirk that I am most definitely already in love with, and says, "Well now, that be the kind o' welcome a man dreams of, it is."

I lazily stretch, thinking I could be a little tempting, when my stomach lets out a loud rumble. He turns to make sure he locked the door behind him and spreads out our breakfast. He brought us bread and cheese, some kind of meat—I will definitely not ask what it is—and some more oranges. I keep the blanket up over me as I sit, and he looks over at me with an eyebrow raised.

"'Tis nothin' I ain't seen, Wench." He walks over to the closet-looking shelf at the end of the bed, and hands me a shirt. I didn't explore there yesterday, so I didn't even realize he had more clothes there. "Go on then, lass. I'll be lettin' ye cover y'self w' me shirt." I think he says he would rather I didn't, but he's already turned back to the table.

The bread was hard today, and I'm not sure how much longer we will be able to eat it or the cheese. I hope he won't bring me moldy cheese. I guess the upside to that would be the penicillin in it, right? I will have to ask Z about that. Oh, right. Since I'm here in the past, I guess I won't be able to ask Z about that. "Will we be able to have fruit every meal?" I ask.

He gives me a small smile. "Ye'll have fruit w' every meal, lass, since it pleases ye so."

I don't understand, though. I remember that they tried to have fruit on ships to prevent some illnesses. Does this mean he isn't having fruit? "Am I eating your fruit? You can't do that! I know that oranges help sailors keep from getting sick. How much are you supposed to eat? We can share—"

He interrupts me quickly. "Ah, lass, no worryin'. I've been makin' sure we've enough to get by o' course. Landfall ain't but a few days off. The crew'll manage jus' fine missin' an apple or orange or two."

Somehow, I know there is more to this than what he's telling me, but how can I question him? He's the captain, for crying out loud, *and* he's keeping me hidden away in his cabin, so it's not like I can even do anything to help aboard this ship.

"Why don't ye tell me 'bout yer family while ye eat?"

The orange slice explodes in my mouth, and with a small smile, I tell him about my sisters.

"Tansy is my older sister by a little more than a year. She is so incredibly strong and brave. She was nineteen when Mama had her accident, and she didn't even hesitate to keep the three of us together. I don't know what all she had to do to make that happen. Azalea was only fifteen, and T had to prove she could provide for us. Mama had a flower shop, Meadow's Garden, and since we had basically worked in it all our lives, T had a good job running her own business. Thankfully, Rod was there to help teach T the business side of things. He has always been a good friend to our family." I smirk at him. "He owns the bar in town, Hornbuckle's. We call it Horney's because that drives him crazy." Serious again, I tell him, "After Mama died, he made sure to always be there for anything we needed. I think I spent as much time at Horney's as I did at home."

I stop talking and realize just how much I already miss my sisters. I know it's only been a few days, but I feel like I have been away from them for years. With a wistful smile, I continue.

"Azalea is a bit wild. She has a larger-than-life personality and is incredibly beautiful. Everyone loves her. When she works with herbs and oils, she becomes completely absorbed in the process, and that's when she is quiet and calm. It's the *only* time she is quiet and calm. She reminds me a lot of my mom. She looks so much like her and absolutely thrives in the Garden."

I shake off the gloom that descends on me, and ask, "What about your family?"

"Ain't much worth tellin', truth be told. Had no parents, not that I remember. Got pressed into the Navy when I was a lad, and I took to it like a fish t' water. The old cap'n saw somethin' in me and taught me the ways of the sea, the pull of the tides, how to read the scripture. Spent years aboard his deck, learnin' more than most ever will. Then one day, our ship was boarded. I had a choice: die with the rest, or live. So, I lived. Bided me time and got me vengeance for the cap'n, and took his place at the helm. That's how I came to carry the title."

I move around to sit on his lap and wrap my arms around his neck. I gently kiss his cheek and whisper, "I'm sorry."

"Ain't nothin' to be sorry over. 'Tis the life I was handed. But now I've you. That's more'n I ever thought I'd get."

He pulls me close and holds me tight. "Will ye stay with me, then? Or be headin' back to the place ye once called home?"

"I don't want to leave you. I don't think I can leave you. You are the other half of my soul, and I don't know if I can take you with me when I go back, so the only choice is for me to stay here. But what will we do?"

"I know well what I'd rather be doin' right now, but the deck won't mind itself. I'll be back in a bit."

With a fast, hard kiss, he turns to leave again. "We'll figure this out, lass. We get through the next few days, that's all. Once we're ashore, we'll make sense of the rest."

CHAPTER 19

TANSY

I tried to sleep on the foldout chair. Honestly, I tried. My brain just won't shut off. I know the rain outside is because I can't settle my nerves.

I don't know what Z is bringing with her. I had no idea Mama kept journals. Why would she have left us letters? This makes absolutely no sense. My anxiety is creeping up, and I know that I have to get it back under control before it becomes more than a light rain. *Why won't Hy wake up? What has she found to keep her from us?*

A message from Z pulls me from my thoughts.

Z: On my way.

Caffeine. I'm going to need lots of caffeine for this.

Me: Bring coffee

Z: Got you

I sigh at her response, imagining the hot cup of coffee in my hands already.

I take a few minutes to check in with Mae. I am so thankful for my closest friend outside of my sisters. Hawthorne is loving spending time with Hayden, and I know I don't need to worry about him.

The door opens, and I nearly jump out of my seat. Azalea walks in with breakfast sandwiches and drinks. I take a big sip. Instead of the hot, strong, bitter taste of coffee I love, I'm met with grassy, lightly bitter matcha. "This is not coffee!"

"T, your anxiety is through the roof. You don't need the caffeine spike to make matters worse. This has a slight calming effect, but still provides the caffeine boost you need. Besides, I made it with oat milk and my special vanilla just because I know it's your favorite."

"C'mon, Z. You know I love your matcha. A warning would have been nice." I open the sandwich and give Z a small smile. "Thank you for making my favorite sandwich." I know it's simple, but I love a scrambled egg sandwich with cream cheese. That's it. Lightly toasted bread with cream cheese and a scrambled egg. Z gives me a small smile in return.

We eat and both move to sit beside Hy, holding her hands. A tear runs down Z's cheek as she leans down to kiss her hand.

"Tansy, I don't understand. Why hasn't she come back yet?" Z quietly asks me.

"I know that I'm the big sister and should be the one with the answers, but I don't have any." I can't pretend to have the answers she's looking for.

The rain comes down harder outside when Doc returns to the room.

"Morning, girls. I'm only a few minutes ahead of the new supervising doctor. Have you noticed any changes in her?"

"No change at all. Azalea found Mama's journals last night. We'll see if we can find something to help. Even if it's just someone who knows more than we do."

WITH A FIRM RAP on the door, a man steps inside. "Good morning, I'm Doctor..." The tall, slender man is very handsome, but he literally freezes in the doorway, staring at Z. His jaw drops, and he runs his hand down his face. He turns to leave without saying another word.

Doc and I stare at Z. Doc asks, "What just happened?"

While I ask, "When did you piss in his Cheerios?"

Z looks at the door, then at Doc. "Is that the new supervising doctor? He walks into a room and rudely turns around to leave? What the hell, Doc?"

Doc looks between us, then gestures toward the door. "Honestly, girls, Dr. Reyes has been completely professional. He has impressed me so far. His bedside manner is a little stiff, but everyone can tell he truly cares about the patients. I was going to ask you girls to let me share Hyacinth's actual history with him. I don't know what that was."

As I start to ask Doc if he was sure, Z explodes, "No! Absolutely, inexcusably not!"

Doc and I look at each other, then back at her. She's shaking. "Um, Azalea, honey, are you okay?"

"Okay, Azalea, I won't read him in unless you say I can. But I need to go find him to see if I can figure out what happened. I'll make sure he understands that since he offended the family, he cannot enter the room without me present. Will that help?"

"He is absolutely not allowed to touch my sister!" Z explodes again.

Doc looks at me, and I shrug. He nods toward Z, then quietly tells me, "I'll see what I can do. I am concerned at this point, though. We need help."

I nod and go over to hold Z's hand as Doc leaves the room. She is still shaking with anger. "Z, honey, what just happened?"

AZALEA

I sit down and put my head in my hands. I have no idea what just happened. The doctor walked in and looked at me as if he had seen a ghost. When he turned to leave, I was instantly angry, but I don't know why. It feels like all my emotions are on hyperdrive. What is wrong with me?

"T, do you think whatever is going on with Hy could be contagious, but only to us? It's storming outside. I definitely had a completely inappropriate reaction to someone. Is this something bad?" I feel like a child asking for reassurance from a bad dream, and I'm sure I sound like it, too. "I felt him come into the room, T. How could I feel him? You and Hy have magic, *real magic*. I don't—I haven't ever felt a person enter a room. Something was going on last night when I found Mama's journals, but this is different. I'm scared."

Tansy wraps her arms around me and rocks. "I won't lie to you. I don't know why you could feel him, but it is odd that he looked at you and ran off." With a sigh, she asks me, "Didn't you tell me you brought some things from that hidden shelf? Let's see what we find out."

I get out the envelopes with our names on them in Mama's flowy writing and hand over the journal. "I didn't read any of it. I looked only to make sure it would be the last one. The date on it is from the week of her wreck. I couldn't read any of this without you and Hy. I know I should have.

Maybe I could have found something that would help us. I'm sorry."

Tansy shushes me. "I think I might have been upset if you had. I don't really want to do this without Hy either, but she is here in a way. We need to find how to bring her back. This could be the only way. So, do we start with the letters or the journal?"

I'm not sure if I'm ready to read my letter. "Let's read the last entry and then decide what to do next."

May 4

The girls are all off to school, but I have a bad feeling. I know they're safe, but it's one of those days I wish I could keep them at home with me. Tansy is almost finished with her first year of college and will be home for the summer soon. I am so ready for all my girls to be back under my roof. My feelings very rarely turn out to be anything at all. But I just can't shake this feeling that something bad is coming.

It's days like this that I wish my Grams were around to teach me about our gifts. I know she taught me all she could in the time we had, but I really miss her. I wish she could see how my girls are thriving. I don't even know where her people are to find them and ask how to help my girls.

Oh well. Being maudlin isn't helping anyone.

*If I don't feel better tomorrow, I'll use
Grams' letter-writing trick. It's always made me
feel better before. Even though I've never sent
those letters anywhere.*

WE BOTH CRY. Tansy gently runs her fingers over the page like she's afraid she will smudge the words. "I remember Mama telling me that when she really needed to say something, she would write a letter. If she still needed to say it after a week, she could send it. If she didn't, then she could burn it. I asked her, 'Why burn it, Mama?' T looked up at me with a soft smile and said, 'Because, Tansy-dear, if I needed to get them out, those words could hurt somebody. Burnin' it keeps all the negative away from all involved.'

"T, that means she wrote us the letters because she still had a bad feeling. I-I don't want to read mine yet. Do you?"

Tansy shakes her head. "I think we may need to read Hyacinth's letter. I've got a feeling there is something in it we need to know. Why else would you have found all this now?"

CHAPTER 20

HYACINTH

*T*he lock clicks into place again. I know I'm not a
prisoner, but it certainly feels like it when he isn't
here. When he brought breakfast, he also brought what
looked like a pail of water. Oh, maybe I can clean up! He has
to have a comb or brush or something I can use to at least get
the tangles out of my hair, although I have no idea where he
would keep it.

I go over to the shelves where he pulled out the shirt I'm
wearing to see if I can find something to use as a rag to clean
up. He has a pair of pants and another shirt in here, as well as
what looks to be a nicer set of clothes. I wonder when he
would need that? There are some rags, and they don't smell
bad, so I'm going to use them. I dunk one in the water. Crap,
that's cold! As I start to take a sponge bath, I realize I'm
feeling sticky. It's saltwater! Ugh! How am I supposed to get
clean? I mean, at least it's better than it was, I guess.

After searching around the room, I still can't find a comb,

or a brush, or anything I can use to get the tangles out of my hair. After finger-combing as best I can, I go through his books. There will hopefully be something to at least hold my attention so that I'm not completely bored, right?

There are a lot of books here. I have found a Bible, a Book of Prayers, an old journal, so many tide charts and star charts, a Book of Omens, and a Pirate's Code. As I'm looking through the stacks, shouting and arguing come from outside the room. I can't hear what they are saying, but they definitely sound angry.

It isn't very long before the key unlocks the door again. I back behind the desk and duck down. What if it's not William? What can I do? I don't even have anything to protect myself!

"Wench? Where ye be?"

I poke my head up from behind the desk, and he laughs at me. He is laughing at me! "Well, what was I supposed to do with everyone fighting out there?!"

He immediately stops laughing. "What d'ye mean, fighting?" Then he mumbles, "We got a mutiny brewin'." *What does he mean a mutiny?*

He snatches up the dagger I found stabbed through a journal yesterday, and hands it to me. "Here, lass. Take it. But know this be a last resort. I'd wager the wind ain't blowin' that foul just yet."

He grabs the chamber pot and water pail and goes back out. Hearing that lock click almost makes me cry. The wind feels like it's picking up, and the sky is getting dark, but it doesn't seem like the whole day should be gone already. Maybe I spent more time looking through the old books than I thought I did.

As the day goes on, the wind picks up more. If I didn't know better, I would blame Tansy for the storm. But there's no way it could be her when she's hundreds of years in the future, right? The ship is creaking and rocking, and I don't feel so good.

I lay down to keep my stomach at least a little settled. I guess I doze off because William wakes me when he comes back in the room. Not even the sight of an orange makes me want to eat, given the way my stomach is feeling by this point. Who knew I would get seasick of all things?

"Breathe slowly, lass. The sea's just tryin' ye on for size."

"I didn't think we were supposed to have bad weather before we got to land?"

"Aye, clear skies all the way, lass. This storm rose outta nowhere, like the sea's got a grudge." *Or my sister does.*

"You need to be on deck with the crew. I'll be fine. I'm just going to stay in bed until the storm passes."

"Ah, lass, I can sit w' ye a bit. Let's get yer hair outta yer face."

He helps me sit and gently pulls my hair back from my face. He runs his fingers through, releasing the knots that have been driving me crazy. Quickly, he braids my hair, tying it off with a bit of his leather string, like the one holding his hair back.

As I lay back down, I ask where he learned to do that. But I don't even hear his answer before someone is banging on the door. He brings over a bottle of rum and tells me to drink a bit before he's quickly gone again.

CHAPTER 21

LIAM

This storm is something else. I get drenched just going from the camper to the back door of the bar. "Mornin', Rod," I say, shaking out my jacket.

He looks up at me and grunts. Ok then.

"Anything you want me to do this morning?" I'm not surprised at getting no answer from him. Based on the dark circles under his eyes and lethargic movements, he didn't sleep last night.

His phone dings with a text. He looks at it, then up at me, trembling. "I have to get to the hospital. The girls-the girls said they need me there. I'm not gonna open today. Just take the day off or somethin'."

His keys are jingling together; he's shaking so hard.

"Hey, man, why don't I drive you up there? I can drop you at the front door, and you can get in there sooner. I don't want to stay in the camper with this storm anyway. So, I'll drive you, then stay in town and bring y'all some lunch in a couple hours."

He just looks at me. I don't know if he even understands what I said. I take the keys from him, and we head toward the hospital. In the car, I remind him to text Al that he's closed today. I'm trying to keep him busy until I can get him to 'his girls'.

TANSY

I don't know what to make of Mama's letter. I don't know whether I'm furious at her for keeping this from us, or if I understand that she just did the best she could.

Rod walks in looking completely devastated.

I push to my feet and meet him halfway across the room. "Oh, come here. I'm so sorry, I didn't mean to scare you!" I apologize as I wrap him in a hug. He holds on like he's waiting for the shoe to drop.

"Um, we need to talk to you about something, and I'm not sure..." I start and he looks down at me, still not saying anything. I lead him over to a chair and nod to Azalea. She hands him the letter.

"Z found Mama's journals last night. When she found them, there were letters for each of us."

He looks down at the envelope, which is addressed to Hyacinth.

"Ok, so? Why are you giving me this?" He asks, perplexed.

"We read it in case there is something that would help us wake Hy up. I promise we wouldn't have read it if we didn't think it could help," Z tells him.

"Tansy-girl, you still haven't told me why you are giving it to me."

Z stands up and walks over to the door. "Rod, you need to

read the letter. Tansy and I are going to get a drink, and we'll be back in a few minutes."

Before I close the door, I glance over my shoulder. He sits there looking at the letter in his hand like it might bite him, before slowly opening it and unfolding the page. I recount what it said, my heart racing as he reads.

Azalea and I don't walk away from the door. We're not sure if Rod will need us, so I didn't want to go far. As soon as he doubled over and sobbed, I texted Doc.

> Me: I think we may need you in Hy's room. She's not awake, but I need to tell you about this.

Gripping my phone, I wait for his response.

> Doc: I hope that means you found something. On my way.

My heart breaks for Rod. He goes to Hy's bed and falls into the chair. He sits with his head on her hand and sobs. Heartbreaking, body shaking, sobs. Over and over, he mumbles, "I'm so sorry. I'm so sorry. I didn't think. I'm so sorry."

Doc speed walks up to us and pauses when he hears Rod in the room. He turns to us, and we quietly tell him what Mama's letter said. His eyes convey his shock. "In all the years I've cared for you girls, she never told me.

My Darling Hyacinth,

There is something important I never told you. If you are reading this, then I never got the courage to tell you.

Please don't blame Rod. He never knew about you.

I fell utterly in love with him when he came into town to visit his uncle. He was getting ready to go into the Air Force and had already enlisted. One touch and there was this shock to my system, and I knew he was meant for me. This big, strong, handsome man and he was mine. I was so confused because he didn't react. We only had a few weeks together, then he was off to some other country. He didn't want to tell me where he was going, only that he would come back to me. Those few magical weeks gave me you. But he didn't come back.

It wasn't until you were almost 2 that I saw him again, but he had someone with him. I don't know what changed. He didn't want me anymore. I didn't think that fate worked that way. I knew he was my mate, but she didn't see fit to make me his. He was so angry and distant that I never had the opportunity to tell him until years had gone by. At that time, I didn't feel like it was fair to tell him and ruin the peace we had found. I hope you can forgive me for not telling you both.

I will love you across all time and space,
Mama

CHAPTER 22

HYACINTH

I wake up alone, but at least the sea seems to be calmer today. It's still overcast, but the wind and waves aren't violent. I sit up slowly, making sure my stomach won't revolt. The good thing about the food not being fresh is what William brought for me last night is still good. There's an apple, an orange, and some kind of jerky. Oh and rum. I know I've been drinking watered-down rum, but I don't have fresh water to dilute this jug with. Oh well. Good thing I like rum.

The door opens, and William comes in looking completely exhausted and gives me a small smile. After locking the door, he pulls me in close and holds me tight.

"Ah, lass, what I'd love t' do t' ye this morn'. I've naught left in me bones but the will t' sleep."

With a saucy smile I say, "I bet I can do something to help you rest better."

I lead him back so that he's leaning against the frame of the bed, and loosen the string that holds his pants up.

He leans down for a fast, hard kiss and whispers, "Well, then, on yer knees, Wench."

Good grief, why did I think I could do this? It seemed like a good idea, but he is *huge*. I guess I stare at it so long that he grabs my hair so that I have to look up at him.

"Damn, ye look like sin itself. But, love, ye don't ha' t' do this."

I look from his eyes, back down, and lick my lips. I can do this. Damn, I want to do this, but I don't know what he likes or really wants. I think he's tired of waiting for me. He reaches down and grabs his cock himself and slowly pumps his fist up and down. I stare at him, completely mesmerized.

"Open yer mouth for me, lass."

So, I do. He barely puts the tip to my lips, and I lick the salty precum off. Oh, I can do this. I replace his hand with mine and then lightly suck just the tip. He hisses out a breath. Well, that is certainly a confidence booster. Deciding that I really can't do this wrong, I keep my hand where his was and pull more of him into my mouth. I tighten my grip and suck, and he groans again. Okay, now, I'm catching on. I realize that between my hand and mouth, I can get a good rhythm going when he reaches down and cups my face. He taps me a bit, so I look up at him.

"'Tis enough, lass, 'less ye want it down yer throat."

I MOAN AND POP OFF. Shocked, I watched him spurt cum across the floor. Oh, my God—that is hot.

He helps me up and finishes taking off his clothes. After removing his borrowed shirt, he tells me, "Into bed w' ye, now." As soon as we are both lying down, he's sound asleep.

I'm snug in his arms, and content to be with him while he gets some much-needed rest.

I wonder what changed that has kept him out there instead of in here with me. What could be changing that has him seemingly worried?

It doesn't feel like long before he's waking up and getting ready to go back out on the deck.

"Is everything okay out there?"

"Me crew is spooked. Seas've turned strange, an' now they're sniffin' 'round for someone to hang it on. I've kept my cabin locked, and now they think the devil's in here."

"How much longer before we get to land? You said it was only a few days, right?"

"Shoulda been a short few days sail, but the storm blew us off course. It'll be several more 'fore we see land."

"Then what do we do?"

"We keep you tucked away, same as before. I stay captain, the crew stays blind, and we don't stir trouble."

CHAPTER 23

AZALEA

I don't know what I thought our letters would say, but I was not expecting that. I'm not sure how this will change things for all of us.

Doc looks at us and says, "Dr. Reyes would like to apologize to you girls. I think y'all should see what he has to say. I want you to think about telling him everything. Knowing what we know now, I want y'all to spend some time with Rod and talk about it. Do y'all need anything from me?"

"Thank you, Doc. We'll talk to Rod and get his thoughts. Can you give us an hour before we talk to Dr. Reyes? I guess we can talk in her room?" I suggest, my anxiety jumping at the thought of talking to this *Reyes* after how I reacted to him earlier.

Doc nods. "I'll be back in a bit. Go take care of Rod. You girls already treat him like your daddy. Make sure he knows y'all aren't gonna change that. He needs to know it."

We walk back into the room, and Tansy goes down on

her knees next to Rod. She whispers, "This changes nothing for us, Rod. Well, that's not true."

He jerks and looks up. "Don't make me walk away, please, Tansy."

I come up behind him and put my hand on his shoulder. "I don't think you understand what Tansy means."

Tansy grins at me, then turns a full smile on him. "You have been a dad to all of us for years. Now it's just official."

"I'm so sorry, girls. I really didn't know. I see it now, but I just didn't know." He hasn't let go of Hy's hand still. "I didn't know. Why didn't she tell me?" He seems to have turned his focus back inward again.

"Rod, we need to talk about what's going on with Hy. Are you okay to talk to us?" I look him in the eye to make sure he can focus on me. If he can't, and after a shock like that, I would understand, then we need to regroup and talk to Dr. Super Whatever later.

Rod straightens and asks, "How can I help? You girls know I'd do anything for all y'all anyway."

TANSY TELLS him about what happened earlier and explains that Dr. Reyes would like to apologize to us. Rod looks angry, and honestly, I won't be surprised if he has a few words for the great doctor himself.

Tansy hesitates and says, "Doc thinks we should tell Dr. Reyes about our gifts. So that he knows exactly what he's dealing with. Rod, she should have come back two days ago." Through the window, lightning lights up the dark sky, and clouds swirl.

Rod looks at her hard. "Settle down there now, Tansy-girl. You know that's not helping. It's enough." My eyes snap up to him, and he's looking straight at T. She takes a deep breath and slowly lets it out. "You know I'm right. You being this upset isn't helping you, Azalea, or Hy. You've got to settle."

LIAM

I'm not sure what I'm walking into here, but I told Rod I would bring them lunch, so here I am. After stopping at the desk to find out where to go, I head to the room. I knock on the door softly so that I don't disturb them inside. Rod is looking hard at the taller woman, and the other one is staring at them with her jaw hanging open.

I knock a little louder and say, "I wasn't sure what to bring everyone for lunch, so I just brought burgers and fries." I nod to Rod and set the food on the small table beside the bed.

Rod looks from me to the ladies and says, "Girls, this is Liam. He's my new bartender, and he brought me up here when you texted. He offered to bring lunch for us. Liam, these are my girls, Tansy and Azalea. Hyacinth is—"

A light knock interrupts whatever else he was about to say. An older doctor steps into the room. "Girls, Dr. Reyes reserved a conference room to talk to you. Are y'all ready?"

Rod gives him a stern look. "Not without me they don't."

The taller sister, I think her name is Tansy, looks startled. "Um, Rod? I don't want to leave Hy alone."

Azalea adds, "Can he come here so we don't have to leave her?"

I don't know why, but I offer, "I'll stay with her."

Rod glares at me for a moment and holds up a finger. "I don't know why you think I would leave my daughter alone with you. Trusting you with my bar is not the same as trusting you with her," he all but growls at me.

Daughter? I thought he said they weren't 'his' girls?

I hold my hands up and back up slowly.

The doctor looks at me quizzically. "There are nurses right here; he can't do anything to hurt her."

The one I think is Tansy says, "Look, I don't know you, but right now, I need someone to stay with her, and I need Rod and Z with me. So, you're it. You do anything out of line, and I'll let Rod do what he will."

I nod. I don't know why it's so important, but I can't seem to leave this room right now.

CHAPTER 24

HYACINTH

*A*s soon as William goes through the cracked door again, someone outside tries to get in. The muffled voice comes through the thick slab of wood. "I'm tellin' ye he got somethin' hidden in that cabin. Somethin' the sea don't take kindly to. This storm? Ain't no natural thing. It's punishment."

The voice eventually fades, but it sounds like things are getting bad out there. I need to keep myself busy, so I decide to clean up the cabin as best I can. I should at least clean up the mess we made. I'm blushing just thinking of it.

Since it doesn't take long to sort of clean up the cabin, I'm left with nothing to do but think. It's getting dark outside again, and I know it's not time for sunset, so I'm guessing the storm is picking back up. Suddenly, the ship tilts and groans, then a loud crack! *What could that have been?*

Raging seas make a good time for some rum. Maybe I can at least knock myself out to sleep through the worst of it.

I creep closer to the door as voices grow louder. "I'm tellin' ye plain, Captain. The crew's desperate to pin this on somethin' or someone. Keepin' that blasted door locked tight only fans the fire. And these extra rations, what in blazes is wrong with ye?"

There's a loud thud and William shouts, "I'll tell ye what's wrong! I'm the bloody captain o' this ship, and if I say the door stays locked, then it stays locked, no questions! And if I want extra rations, then by the Devil's teeth, I'll have 'em! Ain't none o' yer damn business why I do what I do. Now haul yer arse back to deck before I make ye swim with the sharks meself!"

There's another big thud, then the key clicks in the door. As soon as William comes in, I launch myself at him. "This is really bad, isn't it?"

"We lost a mast an' the damned thing swung 'round, crackin' the hull. She's takin' on water. We could still make land yet, if this storm'd jus' quit tryin' t' drag us to the depths."

"What if the storm doesn't let up soon?"

He doesn't answer me, just holds me close. *This ship is going to sink with us on it. I have to figure out a way off.*

"I don't know what to do. At home, a violent storm that came from nowhere would be because Tansy's distraught. Oh, no. Do you think this could be because of my sisters? How can we make it stop? What do we do?"

"Lass, I hate the thought of lettin' you go, but we might have to see you home."

"NO! I'm not going without you. Don't you understand? Our souls are linked. I can't go without you!" My voice rises in pitch and my hands shake.

"This be the only way o' keepin you safe. The crew's restless, and I don't know how much longer I can hold 'em back.

Already kept them from breakin' the lock, love." He kisses the top of my head.

"Crew's a superstitious lot they are. They reckon I'm keepin' the cause o' this cursed storm locked away. If they find ye, we'll both be feedin' the sharks, no doubt. They believe a woman's bad luck at sea. Not 'cause o' the woman herself, but 'cause the sea don't want no rival. She's a jealous thing, the sea, and she'll stir up storms to prove it."

"Then we have to try and go together. There has to be a way for you to come with me. You said the storm isn't normal? What's different?" *This has to be from my sisters trying to help me come home.*

"It ain't natural. The winds spinin' wrong, the sea twistin' in on itself. I ain't seen nothin' like it afore."

Unnatural? Then it's Tansy. It has to be the way.

"Then it has to be the way for us to go together. But if I'm wrong, I don't know what will happen. I haven't tried to stay before. I always wanted to go back home. Maybe the magic is trying to pull me back? That has to be what's right; we should go together."

I can't go back without him, I don't think the FateBond would let me even if I wanted to. If this storm is trying to pull me home, he has to go with me. Nothing else makes sense. I won't go without him.

"Lass, ye said you'd take a nap an' go home when ye stepped through time. But how'm I s'posed to go with ye? How's a man like me meant to follow?"

"The storm has to be the way. You said the sea is twisting? Is it opening up, like a hole? I'm sure if we go together, we will go home. We have to stay together!"

"Aye, lass, a gaping maw, like the sea opened her cursed mouth to drag us under. The ship's not makin' it through."

"Then we have to jump. If we won't survive by staying with the ship anyway, we have to at least try to go!"

He pulls me to him for a rough kiss, the taste of desperation on his lips. "I don' wan' to do this, Wench. If fate sees fit we part this day, and ne'er meet again, the ocean's darkest trenches hold less love than I ha' for ye."

He takes my hand and leads me out to the deck, supporting my weight since the deck is slippery and the wind is blowing me over. I barely hear over the roar of the wind and rain, and my heart beats just as loudly. The deckhands are all busy trying to keep the ship steady. As we approach the side where the whirlpool spins, a crew member with a jagged scar across his eye spots us. With a roar, he charges, and William yells for me to jump. Another deck hand comes around and grabs for me, but William fights him off with his sword. We are almost to the railing when Jagged Scar reaches us with his sword drawn.

William yells he is offering me to the sea to appease her anger, but they won't listen. He's attempting to get me up over the rail when another deckhand dives forward. William steps aside, and the man topples overboard, getting lost in the relentless waves. As soon as William gets me lifted, Jagged Scar is back and aiming for me. William jumps in front of me and tosses me over, just as the sword pierces through him.

I'm falling in slow motion.

I reach for William.

He falls forward and his eyes meet mine. I see the future that can never be, all the 'I love you's' we will never get to say, all the nights we will never get to share. Why would fate give me everything just to let me lose my mate after four days.

I need my sisters.

He was supposed to go back with me.

Tansy gave me a way to get him home.

The vibrance in his green eyes' fades, his expression turning slack. I reach for him, clawing at the emptiness between us, pleading with fate to not let this be the end.

I scream for William, my mate, as I hit the water and am engulfed in darkness.

CHAPTER 25

LIAM

*R*od and the sisters follow the doctor down the hall. Rod told me that this lovely woman is not his daughter, but he just said that she is his daughter. This entire situation is so very confusing.

As I'm wondering what could be going on, she moves a bit. By the time I get to the door to search for a nurse, she's thrashing on the bed, and I can't see anyone in the hall.

It sounds like she is trying to say something. Her voice breaks through. "No, William!"

I rush over and grab her hand as a sudden migraine sends me crashing to the floor. She's crying and looking at me. "What? I... William?"

I try to let go of her hand, but her grip is firm. "Ye—no, I'm Liam. What just happened?" My head throbs with every breath.

She shakes and cries, "No, no, no!"

"Hyacinth, what happened? I don't—C'mon now, love.

Stop yer cryin'." I have no idea where the accent comes from. My head is fuzzy, and it seems like I have memories that are mine, but not. This is so strange. "Come now, love. I need to get the nurse. Yer sisters are worried." *Again with the accent. What the hell?*

She grips my hand harder, "I'm not letting you go, William."

"Hy, love, I'm Liam. I seem to…"

"I said, I'm not letting you go." She levels a glare at me. "I don't know what just happened, but I feel you, so I know you are *my* William. I don't know how or what we are supposed to do. My sisters will help us figure it all out, but I will not let you go."

"A lot seems to have happened while you were sleeping. Your sisters are going to be relieved you're awake again."

"Well, since I wasn't sleeping, they shouldn't have been worried," she says with snark.

I STOP and take a deep breath before I say something I'll regret. This woman won't let go of my hand so I can have someone get her sisters. "Look, Hy, I don't know what all is going on. I truly don't. But snapping at me is not going to help you. Quite frankly, I don't appreciate it."

SHE GLARES at me and points with her free hand. "*You* don't appreciate it? You asshole! I just watched you fucking die!"

I jump up, and she nearly snatches me back down. I look at her grip on my hand. "Can I please at least shift to the other side so I can sit in the chair?"

She softens a bit and takes my other hand in hers, so she is holding both hands, then grins and says, "Sure, just crawl over. I am literally not letting you go."

A laugh escapes me, releasing a lot of the strained tension in the room. I move our hands, so I won't harm her, but still hold on to them. Carefully, I maneuver myself over so I'm sitting on the other side of the bed in the chair and then release the hand that has the IV. I really don't want to hurt her.

"Your sisters and Rod are meeting with a doctor about you. We really should let them know you're awake."

"We can in a few minutes. I just need," she sighs, "a few minutes before they come in and want answers. I don't know what happened, but they'll help us figure it out. I'm sorry, I'm afraid to let you go. William is here, and I'm afraid that if I let go, he'll be gone."

"I DON'T KNOW about that, love." I stop to gather my thoughts as best I can. "First, I don't know why I keep calling you 'love'. I have never done that in my life, so I apologize; it just comes naturally with you, I guess?"

She nods at me to continue, so I go on.

"When I touched your hand, emotions, and it seems like memories, maybe, flooded my mind. I know they aren't mine. I don't know what that means for you, but it's given me a massive headache."

"Please just say you won't leave me? I don't think I can handle losing you twice."

"I don't want to leave you, but when your sisters come back—"

She interrupts, "They will have absolutely no say in you leaving me. As long as you want to stay, I can make them understand you can't leave me." A tear rolls down her cheek. I gently wipe the tear with my thumb and stop mid-motion. *I've done that before.*

· · ·

"I WILL AGREE to stay as long as you want me to. If you let me push the nurse's button to let everyone know you are awake."

She closes her eyes and nods, but still doesn't let go of my hand. I push the button and wait.

"Why were you in my room when I woke up?" I squeeze her hand and tell her, "I brought Rod up here when one of your sisters texted him that he needed to come. I brought them some lunch and offered to stay with you while they had some kind of meeting with the doctors."

"They let you stay with me? Alone?" her eyes big.

"I was at the bar when you fainted. Rod was a little short-handed, so I've been helping out."

"No way Rod let someone he doesn't know help out." She laughs.

The nurse comes into the room and sees that Hy is awake and then rushes back out.

I smile down at her, and she grins up at me. "Well, this is gonna be fun."

IT SEEMS like only a few moments before running footsteps rush down the hall. They freeze in the doorway before racing over to the bed to hug Hyacinth. She still doesn't let go, and the younger sister stares at me. "What did you do to my sister?"

I raise my free hand and shake my head. "I didn't do anything. She did it."

Rod stands in the doorway, glaring at me. The doctor from earlier comes in with a younger doctor. "Well, young lady, it's about time you decided to join us."

CHAPTER 26

HYACINTH

"Well, I didn't exactly decide anything." I look at everyone. I'm certainly a bit fuzzy, but not so much that I can't think straight now. "Why are you all here? And why am I in a hospital instead of at home?"

Rod steps forward while glaring at William and says, "Well, sweetheart, you passed out hard at the bar and..." He runs out of things to say and just looks at me. I don't know what's going on with him, but today is not the day for that puzzle. I can only handle so many things at once, and there are too many people in this room right now.

"I'm sorry, could I speak to my sisters, please?" I look at the doctors and nurses in the room.

The younger doctor steps forward to say, "Well, we need to check you over, so maybe Dr. Harley and I could see you alone for a moment first?"

"Look, I've had a really shit day, and I don't know you. So, the answer right now is, No." I look over at Doc and raise a brow at him.

He says to the new guy, "Dr. Reyes, I explained that she is my patient and a special case. Let's leave her for a few minutes with her family." He turns toward the door and looks back over his shoulder at me. "Young lady, you scared us. I will be back in ten minutes to talk to you and check you over. No arguments."

I still can't believe I'm in my time and holding William's hand. I'm not sure how I'm supposed to tell my sisters that I was trying not to come back to them—well, not alone. I truly wanted to stay with my mate. It's all just so confusing.

Rod has backed up next to the door, but he doesn't look like he's planning to leave anytime soon. I'm not sure why he's here and glaring at *my* William.

Tansy looks at William and asks, "Would you mind leaving us alone with our sister, please?"

I grip his hand as he answers her, "I'll not be leaving her side unless she demands it of me."

Wow, my man just stood up to Tansy. He definitely doesn't know her yet. Lightning strikes outside the window, and Rod steps forward to place a hand on her shoulder. She glances back at him and calms down.

"Doc said he'd give us ten minutes, then be back, so I'm gonna make this ridiculously short to explain. At the bar, I went back in time…to the bar. William found me, and he's my mate. So, let me be clear here. He is not leaving me."

My sisters rush to speak over each other, and I can't even understand what they're saying. Rod hung his head and turned to the door. "I'll just leave you girls be."

Tansy rushed for him, pulling him back into the room. "No, you aren't. You're family too."

I look at Tansy, waiting for an explanation. "T, talk."

"Girl, you are extremely short today! We have been worried out of our minds trying to figure out why you weren't coming back to us. I'm sorry you've had a 'shit day' as you said, but we have had a shit four days. We thought you were gone! Then you come back, and you are rude to everyone, grab onto someone we don't know, and don't even acknowledge that we were worried about you?!"

Thunder rumbles outside as Tansy continues her rant at me. "We have been doing everything we could to figure out how to bring you back to us. We even talked about telling a new doctor about our gifts because we wanted you safe!"

Doc walks back in the door before I could even answer. "Alrighty, everyone out. And I mean everyone!"

I don't let go of my William's hand. I won't. Not until I have to. "Nope. Not happening," I say.

He looks at me, holding tight, and says, "Okay. You want to have this talk in front of everyone, then? I don't think your sisters are comfortable with this whole situation right now."

I nod. He does all the regular checks, including my eyes, blood pressure, and pulse. He asks me if I know my name and the names of my sisters. Of course, everything is fine, so he huffs. "Alrighty then. Liquids tonight, and an easy breakfast tomorrow. If everything is still fine in the morning, I'll let you go home tomorrow afternoon. But I still need to know what happened to make everything so different this time."

"That's the one question I can answer, Doc. I wasn't trying to come back."

LIAM

My head is still pounding, and the noise in this room erupts when Hyacinth said she wasn't trying to come back. I'm trying to let her handle her family herself, but this headache is brutal. Finally, when I can't take it anymore, I tell them all, "Please, can we just breathe a moment?"

This gorgeous woman—yes, she is gorgeous, even in a hospital gown with bedhead—looks up at me with tears in her eyes. I can't take it anymore.

"There is a lot that you all don't know yet. I'm sure that Hy will fill in all the missing pieces for you. I don't think that this hospital room is the place, though. You all know she is medically okay. Can the discussions wait until after she's home tomorrow? I know you all have been up here keeping watch over her for days. Why don't you all go home and get some real rest? Then talk when you are all rested and not—I look at Hyacinth directly—quite so cranky?"

"You callin' me cranky, Captain?" she asks me with a smirk.

"Yes, love, I am, and it's not fair for you to take it out on your sisters when they're exhausted."

Azalea finally speaks up. "I agree we all need some rest, but I don't know that we will get any without knowing what actually happened. You really didn't want to come home, Hy?"

"It's been a bit since Liam brought the lunch nobody ate. Why don't I go find us something to eat, and then we can sit in here and talk while we have some dinner?" Rod suggests.

He looks straight at Hy and says, "Why doesn't Liam come with me so you and your sisters can have a few minutes?"

She's immediately shaking her head no.

"Look, lass, I'll be right back. You need some time with your sisters. They need to know you are okay."

"But what if my William doesn't come back with you?"

I lean down so I can whisper softly to her, "Name me as ye please, lass. I'll always be your Cap'n Dick."

With a soft gasp, her smile lights up the room. "Okay, then. I guess I can let you go. But please don't lock the door on your way out this time."

CHAPTER 27

HYACINTH

*A*s soon as they leave, Tansy and Azalea rush at me. One on each side hugging me.

"We can wait for the details until tomorrow, Hy, but you have got to give us something," Z begs. "We have a lot to tell you, too, you know?"

I reach up to touch my necklace, only to realize that I still don't have it. "Oh no," I cry. "Please tell me one of you has my necklace?"

Both of them shake their heads no. "You probably left it at home when you went to Horney's. It'll be there tomorrow, I'm sure." Z assures me.

T, ever the worrier, pipes in with, "You can't go home alone tomorrow. Until you regain your strength, you need to be with someone. You'll come to my house."

"Ummm, I don't think that will be an issue, T. I'm not letting William get very far. The only reason I let him go with Rod—" Tansy holds up a single finger, but I continue,

"Is because he said something to me that only my William would know. I'm not losing him again."

Tansy looks at me. "You really, truly found your mate?"

"He definitely is. I remember Mama saying that you can feel it when you touch, and it just kept getting stronger. He said he could feel it too."

"How did you bring him back with you? That man is just a drifter who helped Rod out over the weekend."

"Most of it will need to be explained when William is here. I have no idea how I brought him back, and I don't know if he can stay. One of his crew killed him when we were trying to..." I hiccup.

TANSY WRAPS her arms around me in a huge hug. "I'm sure we can figure it out. For tonight, Hawthorne has had fun at Hayden's, but I'd like to snuggle my son and get a good night's sleep. Please, Hy, don't do that again. You scared us."

Azalea adds, "We can explain everything tomorrow, but the quick version is that I found some journals Mama wrote while I was looking for something to help bring you back. I hardly slept at all after finding them. We didn't want to read them until we could all do it together."

"Wait, you said she left us letters? All of us?" They both nod and glance away. "Where's mine? Did you read yours?"

Tansy looks at Z and says, "Well, we hoped yours would tell us something to help you, so we read it. I'm sorry, Hy. We were only trying to help, I promise."

Her rambling tells me there is something big in my letter. I push myself up in the hospital bed, and Z adjusts my pillows. "Can I see it?" I ask, uncertainty making my hands tremble.

Z looks at Tansy and asks her, "Does Rod still have it?"

Tansy takes a deep breath. "I think he does. We should just tell her."

"Tell me what?" I'm nearly pushing to my feet with her tone.

Z nods, and Tansy takes a steadying breath. "Hy, Mama says in the letter that Rod is your father and that he didn't know. We gave him the letter to read today, but then the doctors arrived, and things got chaotic. I'm sorry."

CHAPTER 28

LIAM

$\mathcal{A}$s soon as we are in Rod's truck, he turns to me. "What the hell was that?"

"Rod, if you don't mind, can we go get me something for this headache? Time travel just smacked my brain. I don't know how she did it. I honestly don't, but she brought the other me back with her." It's the only answer I can give him.

I lean my head against the headrest and close my eyes from the bright Florida sun. It's almost sundown, which means everything is still bright, but the visor won't help. Rod stops at the drugstore and tells me to stay put. He comes back out with ibuprofen and hands it to me. "It won't help as much as Z's pain caps, but it might at least take the edge off for you."

The longer I'm away from Hyacinth, the more my head swims and pounds. Rod goes through a drive-through for some fried chicken. "They've had enough burgers. This ain't much better, but at least it's something different."

HYACINTH

I'm staring at Tansy and Azalea. I'm not sure whether or not to believe it. You would think that we would know if he was my dad. He's been a big part of our lives for years, even before Mama's accident. He has always been grumpy, but Mama would have told us something that important, right? How could she not tell me that my father is right here? I mean, I know him. He's the reason Tansy could keep us all together after the wreck. How could he not know?

"Are you okay, Hy?" Z asks. "I have some calming oils and rocks in my bag. Let me get them." She brings a stone with some lavender and something else over to the bedside table. "It's not much, but it should at least help a bit. It might help you rest."

"How could he not know? He's been a part of our lives for years. Why wouldn't she tell us? I don't understand." I'm sure my confusion is clear to my sisters.

"I'm hoping we can find some answers in the journals. You need to know just how hard Rod took the news, Hy. It crushed him. Try to go easy on him." Tansy is ever the peacemaker.

ROD HESITATES in the doorway when they return to the room with dinner. Tansy grabbed my tray from the nurse for me. Yay for chicken broth and gelatin.

For the first time that I can recall in my life, I don't know what to say to Rod. He slowly walks across the room to me. "I'm sorry, Hy, I truly didn't know. Things would've been different if I had known, I swear."

"I know we can't change what's already past. Honestly, there's been enough drama for one day. I will need answers, but for now, we're good? At least until I can go home and we

116

can really talk?" That's all I could think of to say to this man who has been a father figure to me for years, and now I have to reconcile that he honestly is my father.

"Whatever you need, Hyacinth. I just don't want to lose you." He moves away just as Tansy starts asking questions.

"So, Liam, how did you come through time with my sister?"

"Wait!" I exclaim. "Liam, is that your name? I keep thinking of you as my William."

With a roguish smirk that matches the pirate I spent four days with, he replies, "Chief Petty Officer Liam Dougal Keane, retired, at your service, my lady." He bows ever so gallantly before crossing the room to brush a kiss to my forehead. I mean, really. It's like he needed to touch me as badly as I needed him to. It's like I could breathe easier since he came back into the room and is near me again.

"To be honest, I don't know what happened. This morning, I was at Hornbuckle's when Rod got the text to come here, and I drove him. Once I came in, and Hy woke up, she called out, and I was afraid she would hurt herself, so I grabbed her hand. A sharp pain hit my head so hard I almost blacked out and fell to my knees. I remember things that didn't happen to me, but they did. I have my memories, but I also have more. They are all my memories, but then again, they aren't. The only reason I even believe any of this myself is that I know Hyacinth told me—my past self—about her powers. That memory sits beside the memory of serving at the bar the other day. I can clearly see both sets of details."

Everyone in the room stares at Liam. "So, you didn't already know who she was when you came into the bar?" Rod asks.

Liam shakes his head no.

"You had no idea of who I was until you touched my hand?" I'm having a tough time believing that fate somehow found a way to bring my William with me after his crew ran him through with a damn sword.

"I can tell you I was incredibly drawn to you from the moment I first saw you—in a way I've never been before," he says.

A nurse comes in to take my tray and tells everyone that visiting hours are almost over. We all look at her as if she's nuts. "Dr. Harley said to make sure everyone went home tonight so that he wouldn't have more patients," she says with a shrug.

"Y'all go home and sleep! I'm going home tomorrow, and we can figure out everything else then." I hug my sisters a little extra. "I am really sorry that I scared you," I whisper to them.

"You gonna let Liam leave?" Rod asks, but we could all see he already knew the answer.

I open my eyes wide. "Absolutely not!"

He shakes his head and says something low to Liam as he leaves to go home.

CHAPTER 29

LIAM

I'm not surprised Hyacinth doesn't want me to leave. Considering how much worse the headache became when I was away from her long enough to get dinner, I wasn't crazy about the idea of separating from her either.

"TAKE CARE OF HER," Rod growls as he leaves the hospital room.

THE NURSE COMES into the room to settle Hy for the night and raises her eyebrow at me

"I'm stayin'," I state, leaving no room for an argument. She gives a slight nod to the chair and tells me it will fold down into a bed.

. . .

HYACINTH LOOKS at the chair and then at me. She giggles and scoots to the edge of the bed. "I'm so glad she went ahead and got rid of the IV. I need to use the restroom. Can you help me up?" She carefully sits on the edge of the bed. I steady her as she tries to stand. "You need your land legs back, Wench."

Her eyes snap up to mine in shock, then a beautiful smile forms. "I never thought I'd hear you call me a wench again."

Walking with my arm wrapped around her for support, I say, "No ma'am. I don't call you '*a* wench'. I call you Wench. *My* Wench."

I LEAVE her at the door of the ensuite bathroom. Her sisters will need to help her get a shower tomorrow, but it sounds like she is trying to clean up a bit. "Don't you overdo it in there, lass. You still need to recover."

She comes back to me and slides under my arm so that I'm supporting her weight a little more on the way to the bed. Once we're there, she slides to the side after lying down and pats the bed next to her. "I won't sleep if you aren't touching me, so might as well come on in now."

"You need to get some sleep, love. You've had a rough couple of days, especially today." I pull her in close so that she's half on top of me for both of us to fit on the bed.

"I was so afraid I would never see you again," she whispers.

I kiss her temple and recount the memory of my past-self curling around my wench like this before. Except this time there isn't a raging sea rocking us from side to side. It feels right, and I sleep better than I thought I would, considering we're crunched together on a hospital bed.

HYACINTH

I'm not surprised to see Tansy coming into the room already this morning. She stopped by my favorite coffee shop on her way in. They make amazing avocado toast there, and she brought me two orders of it along with an iced caramel macchiato. She pulls out a bacon, egg, and cheese on sourdough and black coffee for Liam. He looks at me. "What, no orange?" He grins.

As soon as we finish our breakfast, Azalea comes strolling in with a big overnight bag, asking when I can go home. "Since Doc hasn't come in yet, I'm not sure," I say.

LIAM TAKES a deep breath and leans over to me. "I need to go to the camper and get a shower. I'm not sure when Rod wants me back at the bar, so I need to stop in and talk to him. Are you okay with my leaving for a while?"

I'm not entirely sure that I want to be away from him. Not yet, anyway. But can I be so needy that he has to be with me every single moment of the day? He must sense the panic rising in me because he leans down and kisses me softly. "I don't have to leave yet. I'll take a walk and call Rod to see if he has a plan for when he wants me back."

Tansy and Azalea look at each other, then look back at me. T says, "Okay, spill!" at the same time Z says, "We've slept now, so talk!"

I laugh at them. "I really missed you guys!"

"Would you guys mind helping me get cleaned up while Liam is out calling Rod?"

They look at each other, then back at me, before jumping into motion. Z brought me a change of clothes and all the essentials. I'm moving a bit slow, but at least I don't need their support to stand and go into the bathroom. I'll wait for a shower until I'm in my own house. After brushing my teeth, I go back out to the room to change into the jeans and T-shirt that Z brought for me. Tansy sits down behind me to brush all the tangles from my hair.

I tell them about William taking me to the brothel to get dressed and sneaking aboard the Cinth. I am just finishing telling them about him bringing me extra fruit when he comes back into the room.

He smiles at me and asks, "Do we need to stop for oranges on the way home?"

Doc comes in as we laugh. "Well, young lady, I'd say you are good to head home today, but Dr. Reyes wants to check you over before we sign you out."

Z immediately cops an attitude. "Why would he even be involved? You are our doctor. He's no one to us."

"Azalea, I don't know why you dislike him, but he is my boss here. He has the right to make sure a comatose patient is okay before going home. And that's what he thinks she is— someone who was in a coma for four days. We hadn't told him about your gifts yet when she woke up, if you'll recall. He is concerned that she is going home too soon."

"Do you know when he will stop by, Doc?" Tansy asks.

"He was in the E.R. when I came in this morning. I don't expect he'll be too far behind me. Azalea, behave yourself. He's a good doctor. Give the man a chance. I'll have the paperwork ready for when he says you can go."

Looking at Azalea, I can tell she's off in another world. "What's up? Why did Doc say that, Z?"

"It's so odd, honestly. I have no idea why I get so prickly when he's near. It's as if I can feel him near me. It's truly uncomfortable to be around him."

I sit up straight and almost shout, "Wait! You can feel him near? Have you touched him? I bet he's your mate!"

"No way in hell is that egotistical…" Her voice trails off as the new doctor comes in.

"Good morning, ladies," he says before turning directly to me. "I wanted to stop in and see your recovery for myself. I've never seen anything like it."

"I've done something similar in the past. It's the first time it has lasted this long, is all. Sorry to have caused concern to everyone. I don't expect it will happen again, to be honest." That's not a lie. I found my mate. Fate sent me back to find William and let me bring him home. What could I possibly ever want to leave for?

"I would like to run a few tests to see if we can figure out what causes—"

Azalea interrupts. "Can't you just let us go home now?"

The doctor shifts at the foot of my bed and glances at Z. "As I was saying, I would like to run a few tests to see if we can figure out what causes your fainting. Being in a coma is not something to be taken lightly, which appears to be the case here. I know you won't consent to more testing now, but at least follow up with Dr. Harley, please," he finishes.

Without waiting for my response, he turns his attention to Z. "I apologize for the first impression I made." He holds his hand out to her, and she takes it. As soon as they touch, they freeze. "I hope you'll allow me to improve that impression, ladies. Hyacinth, Dr. Harley completed your paperwork. Make sure someone is with you for at least the next forty-eight hours."

"What was that?" Tansy asks Z as soon as he is out of the room.

Z stands there, almost frozen in place. "I have no idea, but I swear I just got a shock to my entire system."

"He's your mate. I'm telling you. I felt Liam at Horney's. But when William touched me, it was all over. I knew. He felt it too," I say.

"That's what that means?" T whispers.

CHAPTER 30

LIAM

*O*nce the doctor said we could take Hyacinth home, both Tansy and Azalea started fussing over who was going to drive her and what all Hy would need to take it easy for a few days. I interrupted the discussion. "Excuse me, ladies?"

I don't think I was quite prepared for three sets of hazel eyes to turn on me that quickly. "Could I drive one of your cars? Then you could all go to Hy's house together."

Hyacinth asks, "How's your headache today?"

"Not as bad as yesterday."

Z PLOPS her hands on her hips and levels me with a stare. "And just why didn't you tell me you have a headache? What kind of headache? Is it the pulsing in the base of your skull kind? Or light sensitivity? Or…"

"Hold on, Z. It's like someone is pounding inside my head

trying to get out. Loud noise and light were bothering me yesterday, but staying near Hy kept the worst of it at bay. Today is better, but it's still throbbing. I'll get some ibuprofen and be fine."

All three girls gasp, and Hy laughs lightly. "Z's pain caps will help you so much more than ibuprofen. Thanks to the hangover, I'm not sure if I have any left at home, though."

Z goes digging through her purse and comes up with two capsules. "These should take the edge off a bit, but I don't think it's exactly right for you. I'll think about it and make something that will help better next time you need some."

The nurse arrives with all the discharge paperwork and a wheelchair for us to take Hy home.

"With your head still hurting, you can ride with Hy and me. Z will drive her car, and we can figure out what else we need to do after we get y'all home," Tansy orders.

By the time we arrive at Hy's little bungalow-style house, Tansy decides she will help Hy get a shower, and Z will go to the grocery store. While they take a few minutes to compile a grocery list, I ask if Z would drop me at the bar so I can grab my things and talk to Rod in person. The lunch crowd should be gone, so I can speak to him for a few minutes to see if I still have a job since he was busy when I called earlier. Looks like I'll need it since I'm not leaving.

Rod gives me a nod as I walk in, so I have a seat at the counter. It's the same seat as just a few days ago. Honestly, it feels like a lifetime ago. He hands me a soda and leans on the bar.

"You plannin' on stickin' around then?" he grumbles at me.

"Yes, sir. I'm not leaving. Do I still have a job?"

"Yep. Tucker's been pitchin' in 'til you come back. Think you can start back Thursday?"

I nod at him, not sure what else I can say. "I'll grab my things and see you Thursday, 10?"

He grunts at me, so I assume that's settled. He's already off to take a customer's order.

Since I travel light, my belongings fit on my bike. I get loaded up quickly and get home just in time to help Z unload the groceries.

Woah. Home?

HYACINTH

I know my body has gone through a lot since I was basically comatose, but I did not expect to be this tired from taking a shower. It feels as if all my strength is gone, and I could sleep for another week.

A deep rumble grows louder until it's in front of my house, where it dies out suddenly. Liam's back!

I jump up from the couch and reach the door in time to throw it open for him and Z to come in with their grocery bags. Even with hands full, he gets an arm around me and leans in for a quick kiss.

As quickly as the burst of energy came, it's gone. Liam helps T and Z get the groceries put away, but notices that I'm still standing in the doorway. I haven't even closed the door. He pushes it closed and leads me over to the couch. He sits down and pulls me onto his lap.

"What will it take for me to get you to rest for a while?" he asks quietly.

Before I can answer, T notices us. "What's wrong?"

"Nothing really. I just got overdone, I guess."

"Okay, well then. Z and I are going to leave y'all alone to get a nap. Nap, I said. Understand?" T demands.

With a smirk, Liam replies, "Yes, ma'am."

"Don't you ma'am me! Make sure she rests!" Tansy heads toward the door.

"We will be back, and we both have a key. So, no funny business." Z laughs as she closes the door behind them.

Leaning my head on his shoulder, I sigh. I am exhausted, and it makes no sense at all to me. I've been lying in bed for four days. How can I be tired?

After gently kissing my forehead, he says, "You really need to rest, and I desperately need a shower. Why don't you lie down, and I'll get cleaned up?"

"The better shower is in the master bath. Clean towels are in the closet; you can't miss them."

"Ok, then. Up we go." He lifts me to carry me down the hall.

"You don't need to carry me," as I snuggle into his arms.

He laughs as he stands me by the bed to move the comforter and sheet out of the way. "I may not *need* to, but I certainly like to. In you go."

One more quick kiss, and he goes into the bathroom.

LIAM

I come out of the bathroom and Hy is sound asleep. God, she's beautiful. As I pull her close to me to take a nap, I get a sense of déjà vu.

I held her while she slept the first night. *Ain't nothin' more peaceful than seein' her rest, the world calm 'round her, like it's holdin' its very breath. Ain't sure what brought the wench to me path, but I'll not gi' her back. I'll hold her close and see her safe, e'en if the seas rise against me.*

It feels like coming home to wrap my arms around her to keep her safe while she sleeps.

CHAPTER 31

HYACINTH

*M*mmm. I don't want to wake up yet, not when I'm all snuggled up tight to a seriously firm chest. Liam's hand slowly runs up and down my side, stirring vivid memories of our first night together on the ship.

Does he remember it like I do? Does it feel like yesterday for him, or is it muted, something he can barely relive? Like a blurry image in his mind that he can only pick out bit and pieces.

"I feel you thinking over there, you know," Liam rumbles, his voice thick with sleep. The kind that makes his voice sound three octaves deeper than it normally is.

"I was terrified it was all a dream—that I'd lost you. Even though I still can't make sense of what happened."

"I—" before he can say anything else, Azalea comes in the door, being deliberately loud.

"I'm coming in! Better not be any hanky panky going on!" She laughs.

Liam helps me up with a smile. "Come on then, love. Let's get moving."

I don't think I will ever get tired of hearing that. Or of seeing him in a t-shirt that molds to all those yummy muscles.

Z works on her most incredible lasagna. Mama taught her how to make it, and it's the one thing she makes really well, but it takes a while.

"T IS BRINGING salad stuff to go with the lasagna. Apparently, Tucker keeps bringing her stuff from his garden. It's making her crazy; she doesn't know why he's doing it." Azalea chatters away about all kinds of things while she chops the vegetables to go in her homemade sauce.

"What did Rod have to say when you went to Horney's?" Z asks Liam.

"You know he didn't say much," Liam retorts. "I told him I would be there at ten on Thursday. That way, I have a day here with Hy to keep an eye on her before I go back to work."

"Hmpf. From the way you keep looking her, you'll be doing more than keeping an eye on her." Z laughs.

"Hey now, no picking on my man. At least let him settle in first!" I tease.

"Auntie Hy!" Hawthorne shouts as he races into the house ahead of Tansy.

"There's my favorite Thorny-bug!" I lift him in a swooping hug.

He giggles, "I'm not a bug, Auntie Hy!"

"But you sure are thorny!" We giggle and laugh as I spin and tickle him in our usual hello; it's our own little tradition.

LIAM

Hawthorne stops in the middle of the room. "Who are you?"

"Well, umm…" I look to Hyacinth for guidance.

"He's Auntie Hy's boyfriend," Z singsongs from the kitchen.

"Y'all have got to give Liam a break here!" Hy laughs. "Thorny, this is Liam. Liam, meet my main squeeze, Hawthorne."

I go down on one knee to be closer to his level and extend my hand for him to shake. "It's nice to meet you, Hawthorne."

With a grin, he nods. "You can call me Thorny. All my friends do!" He races off to the kitchen, tugging Hy along behind him.

Tansy pauses beside me as Thorny disappears into the kitchen, her eyes steeling with protectiveness. "My son doesn't take to people very quickly. I can thank his father for that. He takes a long time to warm up to anyone new, and he already accepts you as a friend." With a deep sigh, she continues, "I don't know what happened or how it came to be that you are her mate. I see it, but I don't understand it. I'll take this all at face value for now. But make no mistake, you better not hurt my sister."

As she leaves the room, the air feels charged. It may be my imagination, but I would swear lightning streaks across the sky outside the window.

CHAPTER 32

HYACINTH

*a*fter dinner, Tansy gets Hawthorne situated with his game so that we can all talk about what happened.

"I really am sorry that I scared you guys so badly. I knew that I couldn't leave William behind, and I didn't think I could travel back and forth to keep you all."

Liam growls, "You will not try to go back again."

"Oh, all growly and protective, huh?" Z teases, grinning.

"'Tisn't safe, lass. Swear ye won't go seekin' trouble." Liam grabs me and pulls me into his lap.

Both my sisters stare at him in shock. I wrap my arms tightly around him.

"I promise I will not go looking for trouble. I have everything I need here."

He drops his forehead down to mine. "My head is killing me again. I have pieces of his memories, but sometimes it feels as if William forces his thoughts to the forefront. This can't be real, can it?"

"Z, is there anything you can do to help?" I feel like I'm begging her.

"Let's see if we can figure out what happened. He can't truly be both Liam and William, so his mind needs balance to be restored. Maybe? How often does it happen?" Z is deep in thought, working out the puzzle.

"He had more of the accent coming and going when I first woke up. This is the first time it's happened since we've gotten home, though."

Tansy says, "I remember Mama telling so many fairy tales when we were growing up. It's hard to know which ones are real and which ones aren't. I thought the FateBond was a fairytale. At least until this happened."

"Really? You didn't believe it? I did. I just thought not everyone found their mate. Mama said that if you truly loved someone, and they loved you, too, sometimes fate would smile down on you and give you that bond. I always thought that would be what happened for me until I found William. Or Liam. This is all so confusing!"

Z picks up her purse and heads for the door. "Do y'all think Mama would have written any of the stories in her journals? They're all still at the Garden. I'll go get them and grab something to make tea for Liam while I'm there." She races off, muttering about valerian root and skullcap.

LIAM

Holding Hyacinth eases the headache. I could probably let her get off my lap, but why should I? I like her right where she is.

I know we can't live our lives constantly touching each other. It's only when William literally forces himself forward that the pounding feeling of something trying to burst out of my skull returns. Sometimes, it feels as if a former version of myself possesses me.

"Hyacinth? I have a thought, and I'm not sure I am a rational person saying this. But, is it possible that William is a past version of me? Like reincarnation or something?"

Hy and Tansy both look at each other, then at me, then back to each other.

"I mean, I guess it's not outside the realm of possibility—you do look remarkably alike. We have no idea what brought you with me, except—wait? You died. So maybe? What exactly *do* you remember from the few days I was in the past with you?"

"The memories are hazy. I went into the tavern w' me crew." I shake my head; it's disorienting to remember things with an accent.

"I heard something in the back room and thought we had been found out, but instead, a beautiful temptress was hiding behind a barrel of rum. Took ye to see Scarlet, sorry about that, love."

Hyacinth smirks at me. "Well, she certainly dressed me up fancy."

"Och, that bodice, it molded ye just so."

Tansy clears her throat. "I wish I could've seen your face when you realized he took you to a brothel!" She burst out laughing.

"Seriously, T. I thought my boobs would hit my chin. She had them pushed so high. He couldn't keep his eyes off them!"

"Or me hands, or me lips." I nuzzle into her neck, not caring that her sister is sitting right there.

"Well, now. Ummm. Can we get back to the story, please?" T squeaks.

"We went back to the tavern to look for your—oh shit. Let me up, love."

I can't believe I forgot about the necklace. I grab it from my bag, inside the zipper pocket, and bring it out to her.

"My necklace! I thought it was gone forever!" Hyacinth burst into tears, holding it gently with shaking hands.

"It was in the storage room in the back of the bar. I meant to give it to Rod, but we got busy and ..." She jumps up from the couch, grabs my face, and kisses me hard.

"Thank you, thank you, thank you."

After we sit back down, Hy asks, "Anyway, after we snuck on the boat?"

"Oh, lass, she weren't no boat. That lovely was the Cinth. She were the finest vessel to e'er sail the seas."

Tansy interrupts, "Wait a minute. Who named your boat?"

"Aye, I did, o' course."

"Are you telling me the pirate, who loved his boat more than anything, named his ship Cinth? As in *Hyacinth*?" T asks with her eyebrows raised.

CHAPTER 33

HYACINTH

*I*t's so odd to hear Liam slip between current Liam and past William. He can be in the middle of a sentence, and though his voice will stay the same, the accent shifts.

Even odder still for me is the way our bond feels. It's the same, yet different. If anything, the bond seems to grow stronger now that I'm back in my time. How can the bond be for two men?

"I'm back!" Z comes barreling through the door. "I took a little extra time and made up some capsules that I think might help Liam's head. I only did a few of each of these until we can see for sure that they will help. I'll make more tomorrow in case I need to make any adjustments."

Turning to Liam, she tells him, "These are nighttime only since they could make you drowsy. It's valerian root, skull-cap, and lemon balm. I'm thinking it will ease the ache, quiet your thoughts, and allow you to accept the new memories."

She hands him another pill pouch with a few capsules in it. "These are for tomorrow. Take two as soon as you get up. White willow, lemon balm, and rose for pain, acceptance, and heart. Here's a peppermint oil that I diluted. Rub it into your temples when the pounding is especially bad, but not at night."

Plopping down in the chair with a sigh, she adds, "I think that should make a difference. I thought this would be easier than tea for you."

"How do you come up with all this?" Liam asks her.

"I have studied herbs and tinctures since I was in my teens. It fascinates me. I never stop learning about what they can be used for. I look to the old ways rather than pharmaceuticals whenever possible. Modern medicine definitely has a place and is necessary, but most of the time, natural remedies will work just as well or better without some of the nasty side effects."

"Okay, that makes sense to me, but why did you choose those specific ones for me? You gave reasons for the ones you chose. I don't understand that part of it." Liam seems truly confused.

"Z has an incredible intuition about how to choose which specific herbs and oils to use for each person individually. It's truly her gift. She's studied forever, but it's her insight that makes each one unique," Tansy answers.

Z looks at Tansy as if she were completely crazy. "That's not a gift. It's learned."

"Then why did you choose something for acceptance for Liam? You specifically said you added something to help him accept the new memories?" I ask.

"Just get back to the story. What did I miss?" she demands.

"Super short version is that Liam found my necklace and

William named his boat after me before he ever met me. There. All caught up."

LIAM

"Women weren't supposed to be on the ships. It was a big superstition, but the sailors thought it would bring bad luck and even worse storms. Which, in the case of bringing Hy aboard, it brought a terrible storm, so they weren't exactly wrong."

"That was the last day, but yeah. T, I think you caused a storm to happen a couple hundred years ago," Hy says.

Tansy's jaw drops, and Z huffs a laugh. "Well, we were trying everything possible to bring Hy back."

T shakes her head, "I shouldn't be surprised by anything in this story I guess."

"I KEPT HY HIDDEN AWAY. The locked door alone wouldn't have tipped the crew that something was up. My disappearing to stay in my cabin for hours was very different with extra rations and oranges, however..." I wink and heat rushes to Hy's cheeks.

"The crew did a good job of keeping their suspicions hidden from me until they tried to break into my cabin, and then got my first mate involved. I found Hy hiding behind the desk when she overheard them."

Laughing, she says, "What was I supposed to do? You didn't give me any way to defend myself until after that. I wish I could have kept the dagger. It was beautiful."

"Och, ye shouldna needed it, lass. I failed ye there, love."

"Mommy, I'm tired. Can we go home yet?" Hawthorne has been so quiet, I had forgotten he was here.

"Go pack up your things. We'll leave in just a few minutes," Tansy tells him.

Z suggests, "Okay, tell us the rest so we can try to make sense of things."

"The last day, the storm was horrible. It was spinning like a tornado. The ship was shaking and groaning. There was no way we could have survived if we had stayed, so we decided to jump. Since the storm was definitely not natural, I thought maybe if we jumped together, we might stay together. I thought if the storm was from T, and Z was helping, that would be our way home." Hyacinth explained.

"I WAS TRYIN' to slip us o'er to the rail while the crew was caught up with the Cinth, but one o' the sea dogs saw. After that, it were a matter o' me tossin' Hy over and hearin' her splash. Then the steel o' me first mate, and nothin'."

"Wait, you don't remember going overboard? You fell overboard, I saw you!" Hyacinth was getting upset just remembering.

I lean forward with my head in my hands. Focusing on William's memories has brought the headache back tenfold. Simply opening my eyes is painful.

Hyacinth wraps her arms around me, and sits there a moment before turning to her sisters. "I know we were going to go through the journals, but I think we're done for the night. Can we look through them tomorrow?"

Tansy asks Azalea, "Why don't I take a few home with me to look through before I come into the Garden tomorrow? I can put Thorny down and then read for a bit."

"Why don't I just go to your house for a while?" Z offers. "Then we can discuss what we find, and these two can go to bed. Liam, take the capsules I gave you for tonight. You both need rest, whether you believe it or not," Azalea advised us.

CHAPTER 34

HYACINTH

*T*he quiet that follows my sisters' departure feels peaceful, like the calm that comes after a storm. I hope they can help unravel this; it's been a lot to process in one day. We're still adjusting to William and Liam sort of being the same person.

"Why don't you take the capsules? Then we'll call it a night? I know it's early, but neither of us slept great at the hospital."

"This has been the most insane 2 days of my life. I'm not completely sure this is all happening. Maybe it's a dream," Liam mumbles as we go into the kitchen so he can take the capsules. Thankfully, we cleaned the kitchen when my sisters were still here.

As we get ready for bed, Liam tosses me one of his T-shirts and then walks toward the bathroom. Stopping in the doorway, he turns back to me. "Um...did you want that? You don't have to wear my shirt. I don't even know why I did it."

Laughing, I take it from him. "I don't know if you liked me in the corset or your shirt better."

"My memories of that are very hazy. I think I need to see it all again." He gives me his wink that I love.

"Not tonight, Captain." I grab a pair of comfortable sleep shorts and his T-shirt. "But I will sleep in this."

As he comes back out of the bathroom, he pulls his shirt up and over his head, and I freeze, just staring at him. *He looks so much like William, and now I'm staring at his tattoo. How can he have such a similar tattoo—the compass rose and stars, but with flowers?*

"What's wrong?" His brows furrow, and he quickly lowers his arms. "Hyacinth, what's wrong?"

"Nothing, I…let's get into bed, okay?"

HE FLIPS the light off as I crawl into bed. Once we are settled and I'm all snuggled in his arms, I ask him, "Will you tell me about your tattoo?"

"Oh. Well, when I got out of the Navy, I wanted to get a nautical tattoo. I visited several tattoo shops before finding one that felt right. I told the artist what I wanted, and she showed me a couple of different options. Then, she sketched this for me. The North Star to guide me, a compass rose so I won't get lost, and these flowers. I don't know what they're called, but they called to me."

"Liam, those flowers are hyacinths. You have the same tattoo that William had, but with hyacinth flowers."

LIAM

I pull Hyacinth into me so I can hold her. I don't think I will ever get tired of having my hands on this woman. I feel the bond she's talking about. It's definitely not something I've experienced before.

As we lay in the dark, I'm not ready to give up talking to her just yet.

"What's your favorite color?" I ask, wanting to know *everything* about her.

She pops her head up from my chest to look at me. "What?"

"What's your favorite color?" I repeat, brushing my thumb along her arm.

"Purple. Why?"

"You literally own my soul, but I don't know the simplest of things about you. What's your favorite dessert?"

"Lemon bar cake with cream cheese frosting. Now, you answer both of those questions."

"I haven't really thought about a favorite color. I usually go to grays or black. Dessert though? Chocolate cake with peanut butter icing. Beach or Mountains?"

"I live near the beach. I love listening to the sound of the waves crashing against the shore. It calms me, but I've never been to the mountains. Why the Navy, and why did you retire so young?"

"I grew up in the mountains out west in the foster care system and enlisted as soon as I could. I knew it was the only real chance I had to make something of myself, and nothing was holding me there."

Hy props her head in her hand to look at me while she listens.

"There was something about the sea that called to me. I felt like I belonged there. I worked hard and rose through the ranks. I planned to stay in at least the twenty years. I loved everything about it—the brotherhood, the discipline, the adventure, and the feeling of making a difference. My team and I were sent out on a counter-piracy op. Our intel wasn't complete, and we got into a firefight. I took a hit, but my men secured the remaining pirates, and all other injuries were minor."

Hy pulls in even closer to me and traces the scar on my abdomen. "Is this from that mission?"

"Yeah," I tell her around a yawn. "I was medically retired after recovery."

"Wait—you and William were both struck by a pirate, him with a sword and you with a gun." She asks, and I glance at the raised pink skin above my belly button.

HYACINTH

That injury must have been severe for the Navy to medically retire Liam. It would mean that he couldn't continue to perform at the level required to do his job.

My thoughts race, running wild with what it all means for him.

"Stop thinking so hard, love. We'll face tomorrow, tomorrow," he says as he rolls to hover over me.

Leaning down, his free hand slides through my hair as he softly kisses me. I reach up and grab hold. I'm not letting him get away so gently. I want a real kiss. I want to know that he is with me.

He leans his forehead against mine, breathing heavily. "You need to rest, lass."

With a sigh, I turn so his arms are wrapped around me, and I'm snuggled in close. He slides his hand under the T-shirt, his hand burning against my skin, and kisses the top of my head before settling behind me.

He relaxes into sleep behind me fairly quickly. My mind won't shut down to rest. I keep going back to something Z said earlier about the capsules she made for him. They all had to do with pain for the headaches, but then she said something about quieting his mind and accepting the new memories.

I know she's onto something, but I don't know what we have to do for him to be okay. There are so many similarities between William and Liam that I feel he's right in thinking it has something to do with a reincarnation type of thing.

What if bringing William with me is too much for Liam's mind?

What if he wakes up tomorrow and forgets everything, and then we lose the bond?

What if William completely takes over and Liam is gone?

What if—there are too many what-ifs.

I fall into a troubled sleep as I try to grasp a memory that floats just outside where I can grab hold, something about hearts and minds being tangled together.

CHAPTER 35

HYACINTH

I wake slowly to realize Liam's hand is on my breast, and he's awake. As soon as he realizes I'm awake as well, he slides his thumb back and forth across the nipple.

"Good morning, Wench."

"Mmmm. Morning."

I can definitely appreciate waking up this way. I start to roll over to face him, but he tightens his arms, so I stay enclosed in his embrace with my back to him. He slightly shifts the t-shirt so he can kiss my shoulder.

With his arm pinned in place beneath me, he keeps that hand occupied with massaging and pinching my nipple. His free hand slides inside my sleep shorts to tease and play with my clit.

I throw my head back to rest against his shoulder, so it's pinned between his head and the pillow. I moan when he slides two fingers inside me. He's moving his fingers tortuously slowly as I buck against his hand, trying to get the friction I want. He chuckles softly as he bites down on my shoulder to hold me still.

"Easy, love, we'll get you there."

Shifting his hand so he can increase the pressure, he adds a finger and grinds the heel of his hand on my clit. I scream as I come unglued, and my back bows away from him.

He slides back, and I can roll onto my back while he slides my shorts and panties off. He pulls me forward so that I'm sitting up. "As much as I like seeing you in my shirt, I'd really like to see you out of it now."

As soon as it's off, he pushes me back down. After dropping a quick, and completely unsatisfying, kiss, he sits up. He stares without touching me for so long that I reach for him. He takes both of my hands and moves them to the side. "I swear, Wench, you are a veritable feast for the eyes."

He gently glides one finger down the side of my body, starting at my shoulder and ending with my foot. I would never have dreamed that could feel so very erotic. "Liam, please."

"Please you? You greedy wench, of course I will."

Lifting my foot, he kisses all the way up my leg before draping it over his shoulder. "I've dreamed of you, you know. Since the first time I saw you in the bar." Speaking softly while he moves my other leg so that both legs are over his broad shoulders, and I'm spread open for him.

"I felt like the most depraved of men lusting after you while you were in the hospital." Dipping his head low, he blows gently, and I hiss at him.

One long, slow lick, and I reach down to grab his hair. With a devilish smile, he says, "Ah, lass, this is a view I will ne'er grow bored of."

He dives down for another taste, and I'm completely incoherent. I have no idea what I'm saying or what noises I'm making. He chuckles as he uses his tongue and teeth to torture me.

"Nay, love, 'tis not torture. That'll come later." He eases his fingers back inside while he sucks on my clit.

"Come for me, Hyacinth," as he bites down.

Just that quickly, and I'm screaming through another orgasm.

LIAM

Her screaming my name has got to be one of the most satisfying sounds I have ever heard in my life. I think it will become my life's mission to hear it every day.

I shift so that I can kiss this incredible woman. Grabbing hold of her hair with both hands, I devour her mouth much like I just ate her pussy.

"I don't know which flavor of you I like more. I may have to do several recon missions to discover the truth of it."

Hyacinth sighs, "I'll gladly assist in the intelligence gathering."

"Hy, please tell me you have a condom here."

Her face falls. "I… don't. I don't exactly have many…um. Liam, I'm sorry."

"We'll talk later about protection, but I'm not risking you getting pregnant until we are ready for that, okay?"

She goes still and whispers, "I don't want to be finished."

"Och, lass, I've got the thing." I stand and remove my shorts that I hadn't taken off, knowing I would take her if I did.

Her eyes go big, and she reaches for me to wrap her fingers around my shaft gently. I let her touch and explore for a moment before I stop her.

"Do ye trust me, love?" She looks up and nods. *Again with the pirate, this is* my *time with Hy.*

"Turn so your head hangs off the edge." She scrambles to follow my instructions. God, this woman is a gift. Her hair spread out fanning beautifully, her eyes on me, well, a part of me that reaches for her as well.

I clear my throat at this gorgeous sight. I reach for her hands and hold them tight. "Hy, I need you to listen, so look up at my eyes." Once she does, I say, "I'm going to need you to tap my thighs if this gets to be too much. Can you do that?"

She looks back down at my cock and licks her lips.

"Hy, you need to answer me, love. I need to know I won't hurt you."

She shakes her head. "You won't hurt me, but I don't understand what you want me to do."

I STEP FORWARD so the tip of my cock is almost touching her. Taking her hands and placing them on the outside of my thighs, I tell her. "Tap my thighs with your hands, love."

Never moving her eyes, she squeezes my thighs. Taking the tip of my cock and rubbing lightly against her lips, I chastise, "That's not tapping, love."

She quickly licks the precum off the tip as I step back. She mewls at me with a pout.

"Want to try again? Can you tap my thighs?"

Quickly nodding, she places her hands back on my thighs as I step forward. Touching the tip to her lips again, she licks me and taps both hands.

"If you need me to stop, you have to tap, okay?" She sucks the tip into her mouth and nods so that I move with her and squeezes my thighs.

I lean forward and palm both breasts as I slide further into her warm mouth. God, this is incredible.

"Hy, I need to know you are with me, okay? Squeeze if you're good, tap if it's too much." And I shove my dick as deep and hard as I can.

She taps both hands, and I step back.

"THANK YOU, HY." I smile down at my wench, brushing my thumb along her chin.

"For what? I failed. I made you stop."

"You let me know it was too much. You have to know you're in control, understand?"

She nods and reaches to pull me in close again.

"You sure, love?" I ask, desperately wanting her lips wrapped around my cock again. She squeezes my thighs as I rub the tip against her lips again.

With a smirk, she takes me as deep as she can, and I jerk forward. She moans around me as I brace myself on the headboard and hang my head to catch my breath.

Giving her a moment to set the rhythm, I play with both nipples, and she gasps. I pause, so she squeezes my thighs.

She is so responsive. I mold her breasts and tease her nipples until they are stiff peaks. I know I won't be able to hold off much longer, so I pinch both peaks to get her attention. Again, she squeezes my thighs, but adds a twist of her tongue and a moan that sends vibrations through me.

Once I know she's good, I order, "Spread yer legs, love." She immediately drops them open for me, and I dive right in to feast and play with my obsession—that bundle of nerves that drives her wild.

CHAPTER 36

HYACINTH

I grip Liam's thighs as a shudder runs through my body. He's already given me two orgasms today. How can I possibly have another?

I thought this was supposed to be about making him feel good.

How am I supposed to do that when he's making me feel this good?

I didn't even know this was possible.

HIS ALREADY LARGE dick gets even bigger, so I'm sure he's about to come as well.

"Hy, love, I need t' know if ye want it down yer throat."

I hesitate, and he goes still. I lightly tap his thigh.

He slowly shifts his hips as he gives one last lick to my pussy and blows a breath that causes me to shudder. A quick pinch of my clit with a fast pump of his fingers, and I'm over the edge again.

. . .

HE LETS me ride it out on his fingers before stepping back and taking hold of his cock with the hand that still has my juices running down it. Two jerks of his fist, and he paints my chest with his cum.

As my heartbeat slows back to normal, I shift so that my head is on my bed. Eye level with his softening cock, I just stare. I don't even know what to say after that experience.

He leans forward and smears the cum around my chest. "I wanted t' paint yer chest since the first time I saw ye burstin' the seams of yer top." He gives himself a slight shake. "Don't move, love."

I don't think I could move even if I wanted to. My body is as limp as a well-cooked noodle.

LIAM

She has an oversized tub in her bathroom, and we worked some muscles that will be sore for her. I get the bath running and grab a rag to clean most of my mess off her before I bring her in here.

I feel her stare as I walk away to drop the dirty rag in the hamper and add the bubble bath I found under the sink.

I lift her from the bed with a slight grunt. I'm sure I'll pay for it later, thanks to my injury.

"I'm too heavy, put me down."

I snarl at her, "You are not too heavy. I lifted you wrong." Eventually, she will come to understand that she is perfection. I plan to worship her body every day until she knows it without any doubt.

Gently, I set her in the bubble-filled tub. "I'll be back in a bit."

. . .

GRABBING my bag for fresh clothes, I head down the hall for the other bathroom. I don't think she plans to go anywhere today, so after I shower, I pull on my sweatpants and don't bother with anything else.

Heading into the kitchen, I take the capsules Z left for me. She said to take them first thing in the morning, and this is close enough. While Hy relaxes in the tub, I start breakfast for us.

Cheesy egg bake is super easy and can take care of itself in the oven. Once that's cooking, I start some coffee.

Last on my mental list is changing the sheets on her bed. I made quite a mess of them, and I saw where she keeps the clean sheets when I grabbed towels yesterday.

HYACINTH

I hear him moving all over my house. What could he possibly be doing when he could be in this glorious tub with me?

Finally, he comes back, dressed in—God help me—gray sweatpants. I never understood the appeal of sweatpants until this moment, with them hanging low on his hips.

He stops in front of me, smirking. "Like what ye see, do ye?"

Crossing my arms just right, lifting my boobs all the way out of the water, I push them together. "Do you?"

The towel he was holding falls from his hands to the floor. He slowly gets down on his knees and leans forward. Taking both breasts in his hands, he lifts one to his mouth and sucks hard. Then repeats the process on the other. Straightening up, he admires his work, my nipples hard and aching.

"Absolute perfection, Wench." Leaning forward again, he pulls the plug on the tub and drops a quick kiss to my forehead.

"Up w' ye. Time t' break our fast." Picking the towel back up, he assists me in stepping out of the tub and wraps it around me, tucking the end in. Shaking his head, he mumbles, "Such a shame to cover up. I'll leave you to get dressed. God knows if I stay in here with you, it won't happen."

I look around my room for his t-shirt, which I slept in, but the entire room is already picked up, including my bed, which is made. Since I can't wear his shirt, I need to find something that will still drive him crazy. I know just the thing!

CHAPTER 37

LIAM

*W*hile I wait for Hyacinth to get dressed, I plate the eggs and section off one of the oranges from the counter. After getting it all on the table, I grab two mugs from the cabinet, realizing I have no idea how she takes her coffee.

Fuck me. She comes around the corner in a tank top and short shorts. I'm pretty sure that's all she has on. *That might be better than the corset.*

I'm standing there dumbfounded in her kitchen, with an empty coffee mug in my hand, trying to remember what I was doing before she walked in.

"LIKE WHAT YOU SEE, CAPTAIN?" She steps forward and takes the cup from my hand, grazing my arm with her breast.

Wrapping my arms around her, effectively trapping her

against the cabinets, I lean down and nuzzle her neck. "I love what I see, Wench. Want me to prove it again?"

Laughing, she steps away from me. "Absolutely, I want you to prove it to me several more times today. But first, we eat."

AFTER FIXING up her coffee with just a little creamer, she turns to the table. "You cooked?"

"It's basically just scrambled eggs with cheese. I baked it in the oven so that it would be ready when you were finished with your bath."

We eat fairly quickly and get the kitchen cleaned back up before she turns to me with questions in her eyes. "How's the headache?"

"Not bad as long as I'm touching you. Sofa or bed? I'm going to hold you while we talk either way."

With a smile that could light the night sky, she says, "Bed." She leads the way down the hall.

BEFORE WE STEP into her room, she stops. With her hands on her hips. "Where are your clothes?"

"Oh. I, uh, put my bag down the hall while you were in the bath. Why?"

"You can bring them back in here, please." It's apparent that this is a demand, not a request, so I go down the hall and grab the bag to bring with me.

As soon as I step into her room, her hand is held out, palm up. "Yes?" I feel a little silly asking.

"I'll take one of those shirts now."

Smiling, I grab one of my last two clean shirts and hand it to her. "Where would you like my bag since you don't want it down the hall?"

. . .

THAT WENCH HAS TURNED her back to me and is stripping her tank top over her head.

"Stop," I growl at her. She has just bent to remove her shorts and freezes. Those glorious breasts hanging ripe for my picking. Her head turns slowly toward me, a teasing grin on her face. "Yes?"

Dropping my bag, I step behind her, fill both hands, and groan. "We cannot spend the entire day fooling around, Wench."

"You are correct. We cannot spend the entire day fooling around. We can, however, spend the entire morning fooling around." She wiggles her ass right up against my already hard cock. "And I did the math. My next cycle should start in just a few days."

THAT'S all it took for me to yank her ass up against me so she could feel just exactly what she does to me. "Spell it out, love. What are you saying?"

"I want you to fuck me, Captain. I'm assuming you're clean after all the testing from the injury?"

"I'm clean, lass. Havna' been w' anyone since well before then e'en." My voice is all but gone, and my brain can't decide which version of me to use.

"Well, then, Captain. I want you to fuck me, and I want you to fuck me bare."

CHAPTER 38

HYACINTH

"*I* don' think this is gonna be slow or easy, love."

Reaching behind me, I fist him through the sweats. "I don't particularly care right this second. Slow and easy can be next time."

He rips my shorts off and leans me over the bed. Shoving one of my legs aside with his foot so that I'm open to him, he thrusts three fingers in to make sure I'm ready, but I'm dripping for him from the anticipation alone.

"God, lass. 'Tis all for me." No question in that, just a statement that he knows I'm his.

ONE MORE PASS with his fingers, then he lines his cock up. He doesn't even take the sweats off, just shoves them down a little.

One swift thrust, and he's seated to the hilt. "God, love. So tight." He doesn't move to allow me to adjust.

"You're too big. I'm too full." It's almost painful, but so good at the same time.

"EASY, love. You're made for me. Just relax and give it a moment. You and I are a perfect fit." He's being so patient with me, when I know it's hard for him. His legs are shaking from the control he's using.

He eases out slightly and rocks back in a few times until I'm moving with him. "You ready, Wench?"

"God yes, Liam."

He grips my hips and pulls almost all the way out before slamming back into me.

"Not gonna last this time, love. Need you to come already." He reaches around and plays with my clit while slamming all the way inside, and I scream his name as I do.

Two pumps later, he jerks inside me as he shouts his own release.

We both collapse forward on the bed, breathing heavily. He pulls back a bit, and his cum runs down my leg.

"Be right back. Don't move, or there will be a mess." He grabs a warm rag from the bathroom and gently cleans between my thighs before scooping me up and placing me on the bed.

LIAM

"Sorry, love," I tell her as I remove the sweats and crawl into the bed next to her.

"What are you sorry for?" she asks, sounding confused.

"Didn't mean to be so rough with you," I tell her as I draw her into my arms and place a kiss on the top of her head.

She snuggles in close and says around a yawn, "I'm not fragile, you know."

Running my hand up and down her arm, I get another sense of déjà vu. In a feeling of familiarity, I know that I've held her this way before. The echo of William's memories flickers in my mind. Almost as if he chooses which pieces of the memory to share with me.

"How's your headache?" she whispers to me.

"It's not bad, honestly. I think the capsules Z gave me may have made a difference. Along with all the TLC I'm getting from a certain foxy wench."

"I've been thinking about what you said. If this is a form of reincarnation, then William is a former version of you. Right? Does that make sense? I mean, since we don't really know anything about this, we have to follow the illogical logic." She laughs lightly at her word choice.

"What I know is the closer you and I get, the less my head hurts. It isn't logical that when I speak, I sound like myself one minute and William the next. But I understand what you're saying. In some weird way, it makes sense." I shift so that I have both arms wrapped around her.

"William didn't share all of his memories with me. This is the first time I have made love to you, and I didn't actually know what you looked like in the corset until we were talking last night. It was like he was concerned for your safety, so he forced himself forward. He didn't share his feelings for you. I think he gave me the memories he felt I would need, but nothing more."

"I can't say I'm upset about that. I had four days with him in the past. After three days in the present—my time, with you—the bond already feels more substantial, more tangible. I wish we could find someone to ask, but we haven't found that person yet. So, we'll figure it out as we go. As long as we're together, we can do it."

"I'm going to enjoy exploring every inch of this glorious body. Over and over again." I am definitely enjoying punctuating every one of those words with a kiss, working my way over her body to show her just how much I appreciate this body.

CHAPTER 39

HYACINTH

*L*iam is running another bath for me. He wants to make sure I'm not too sore from all our morning activities, and I won't disagree. I could definitely get used to all this pampering. This time, I hope he'll get in with me.

He comes back to the bed and reaches out his hand. I move toward him, but don't let him slide his arms under to pick me up again. He scowls at me, but I hold his hand and pull him with me. After I get in, I slide forward and look up at him, waiting to see if he'll take the hint.

With a sigh, he steps in behind me and settles in. "The idea is for you to relax. It's hard for you to do that if my boner is jabbing your backside."

I giggle at his nonsense. I bite my bottom lip and lean back into him. He wasn't kidding. "Can you relax while you watch my boobs float in the water? I can make them play peek-a-boo with the bubbles if you like."

He reaches around me and completely covers both of them with his big hands. "No playing peek-a-boo this time. Your body needs a break."

"Liam, you massaging them won't help me relax." I laugh.

"I beg to differ. Massage absolutely helps relaxation." He tips his head and places a kiss on my neck, but he doesn't let go. "I can't seem to help myself. You are absolutely gorgeous, and naked is my favorite way for you to be. Unless you're in my shirt, that's a close second."

I lean back and relax against him. He adjusts his arms to encircle me. I know there are more things we need to figure out. Still, I'm going to take five minutes of peace here and now.

He starts to ask me something, but I turn my head to kiss his lips lightly. "Five minutes. I want just five minutes of us being together without worrying about a problem. I have found my FateBond mate. The one person fate herself deemed *me* perfect for. I want to appreciate what we have for just five minutes. Please?"

"Answer one question for me; then I'll give you all the time you want," Liam says. "When are your sisters coming back?"

With a shocked laugh, I answer him, "They close the Garden at two. Z will come straight here, but T will go pick up Thorny before she comes. Then we can solve the world's problems as a family. Until then, we can be a not-so-normal couple who already know each other better than most ever will."

LIAM

We will have a few more hours to ourselves. As Hyacinth put it, to be a not-so-normal couple.

"What's your favorite flower?" I ask her.

Hy laughs. "This again? I know most people would think it's hyacinth, and I do like them. My favorite is a hydrangea. I love the way they resemble a little bouquet and come in so many colors. Your turn."

I start slowly massaging her neck, pressing my thumb into the muscles. "Mine is hyacinth. I didn't know its name when I got my tattoo, but I've always loved it. Favorite soda?"

She moans and drops her head forward while she answers. "Coca-Cola if I have to have soda, but I prefer sweet tea. What's your favorite drink?"

"I generally go for a beer, and I like to find small breweries. Alcohol, I go for rum and Coke most of the time. I won't drink much of it, though. I typically have just one beer if I'm going to have anything."

"I usually go for a rum runner or a rum and Coke." Turning slightly so she can look back at me, "Why don't you drink much? Not that I'm judging your lack of drinking; I rarely drink more than one either."

I raise my eyebrow at her.

Laughing, she answers the unspoken question. "We were celebrating Tansy's 30th birthday. I absolutely got drunk that night and had the hangover to prove it the next day." Her tone shifts to seriousness. "However, I don't think that's why I time-traveled. I think that happened because you came into the bar, and I was supposed to meet William first."

Water splashes as she turns back around and leans against me again. "I'm going to come back to that and answer your question first. I don't drink a lot because it can cause stomach problems, thanks to my injury. I also don't eat spicy foods for the same reason. I can lift heavy things if I do it correctly, but I have to be careful. For instance, I can easily lift a case of beer at the bar. If I want to lift a keg, I have to do it the right way, or I could injure myself." I tell her.

I press a kiss to her shoulder, "If I'm right, and William is a past version of myself, it would make sense that you had to meet him before actually meeting me, especially if, as you say, fate was at work. I was really drawn to you that day in the bar. I couldn't take my eyes off you."

Her hands don't stop moving across my arms that are wrapped around her. "I couldn't see your face clearly; you were turned just enough that your features were hidden. But your voice felt familiar. Maybe that was the bond trying to draw us together, but it couldn't, because I hadn't met William yet. I know this doesn't make sense."

She shifts and taps my bicep, "William had a tattoo of a kraken here—a huge sea monster."

I laugh, "I think you've seen my kraken already this morning."

The water is starting to cool, and we should get dressed for when her sisters get here. "Let's get out and get some lunch. A lusty wench I know has made me work up quite an appetite."

CHAPTER 40

HYACINTH

*A*fter a quick lunch, Liam asks. "You said the Garden doesn't close until two, right?"

"Yeah?"

"I want to show you a piece of my world." Grabbing my ass, he tells me, "As much as I love you in a skirt, you'll need jeans for this."

After changing, he leads me out to his bike. "I've never ridden," I admit, both terrified and exhilarated at the thought of riding on the back of his bike.

"It'll look even better with you on the back." He grabs his helmet, placing it on my head with a wink. "I only have mine, but you'll wear it today. We'll get you one before the next ride."

I'm filled with unease and excitement. It's something I've never really thought about doing, but it's giving me a glimpse into a side of Liam I have yet to explore. As he tightens the helmet strap, he gives it a quick tug, a smirk pulling at one corner of his mouth. He leans down, planting a quick peck on my lips.

He turns away from me, stalks to his bike, and gives me a 'you coming or what look.' Watching him mount his bike was mesmerizing. I couldn't look away as he threw his leg over the seat, the movement practiced and smooth. His little smirk tells me he knows I was watching. It's sexy as hell seeing him like this, and he knows it. He starts the engine, revving the motor slightly, showing off how powerful both he and the machine are.

He motions me over, his voice low and sure. "Throw your leg over and wrap your arms around me. You'll want to hold tight." He taps the foot pegs, where my feet go, ensuring I won't be in his way or get hurt.

Without warning, he launches us forward. With a shriek, half laugh and half scream, I lock my arms tight around him. His laugh rings out as he eases back on the throttle to settle us into a steady rhythm. I'm not about to loosen my hold, keeping myself completely plastered against his back.

LIAM

The bike vibrates beneath me, a steady hum that's familiar and exhilarating. I don't plan for us to be gone long. I know she has to be tender from this morning, and those same vibrations could increase her discomfort.

Her arms are wrapped tightly around my waist, my borrowed helmet digging into my back. She's holding on like I'm the only steady thing in the world, and damn if that doesn't make me feel untouchable.

I turn so that we are on the two-lane road that runs next to the beach. The sun glints off the ocean, but I can't hear the waves crashing over the roar of the engine. Wind whips past us, bringing the scent of saltwater brine with it.

Her grip tightens as I increase our speed, and her laughter rings out, surrounding me. Every mile feels like a stolen moment in time. I know we have to go back to reality and face our uncertainties all too soon.

In this moment, it's not just about the freedom of the ride or the pull of the horizon. It's about the woman who climbed on behind me, the woman I'd chase through every lifetime if I had to. The girl of my dreams, holding me like she already knows I'll never let her go.

CHAPTER 41

HYACINTH

*A*zalea waltzes in the door, singing 'I'm Walkin' on Sunshine' at the top of her lungs.

"Z, honey, did you have a good day at the Garden?" I ask while Liam laughs at her theatrics.

"Did I ever! Before T gets here, I have to tell you. Tucker came in again. He brought her more things from his garden, and Tansy talked to him for at least 10 minutes! Tansy and Tucker sittin' in a tree…"

"Whoa. Wait, a minute. You know he took her home from her party, right?"

"No! But he brings her stuff every day." More seriously, she adds, "He made her cry. She thought he was trying to tell her she's fat or some such bullshit. I'm telling you, if he brings her more vegetables, I'm going to tell him to stop trying to shame her."

"Um, ladies, maybe he just doesn't want to bring a florist flowers?" Liam adds.

I realize Z and I are still standing in front of the door, and Liam has gone to sit on the couch in the living room. We both join him. I snuggle next to Liam, and Z walks toward the kitchen.

"I'm grabbing a soda, want anything?"

LIAM LEANS CLOSE to my ear. "She does know this is your house, right? Or do you all do this at each other's homes?" He seems genuinely confused by how at ease and comfortable she is in my house.

"We've always been this way. Even when most sisters go through the fighting or 'I hate you' phase, we never did. We have keys to each other's homes. I'm sure that's why she came in singing so loudly. She wanted to warn us in case we were…you know…." I blush bright red.

He pulls me into his lap and whispers, "Want me to let her interrupt something now?" Nuzzling me, he teases along my neck when she comes back into the room.

"Yuck! C'mon, guys, really? I was only gone two minutes," Z jokes.

Liam keeps me pinned on his lap with his hands on my hips. "You know I can sit next to you, right? I don't have to use you for a chair; there's a perfectly good couch cushion right there." I point beside us.

"I like you sitting just where you are," he says, simply.

"Okay, but seriously now, is that just a thing with you, Liam? Or does that help your headache? And how bad has the headache been today?" Z asks.

BEFORE HE CAN RESPOND, Tansy walks in talking on her phone. "I don't care that you have some big event. You don't get to just change the night you are taking our son without talking to me first. Your parents have promised him some fun thing to do tomorrow, and he's going to miss school and stay over an extra night. That's not what we agreed to!"

She finally looks up at us. "Douche is an asshole," she says, holding the phone away from her ear. "Hello? He-Hello?" She checks her phone and huffs. "He hung up on me!" Inelegantly, she flops herself into the chair by Z. "So, what did I miss?"

"Wow, T," Z says. "That was quite an entrance. Dr. Douche picked up Thorny from school without letting you know again?"

"Yep." Tansy says, popping her 'p'. "He thinks he can do whatever he wants, whenever he wants, just like when we were married." She sighs. "And he's not wrong. It's not like I can take him back to court. I can't afford that. Anyway. Enough about his bullshit, I'm done with it for the day. Hy, I'm raiding your wine. When I get back, y'all will catch me up, understood?"

LIAM ASKS, "Do I want to know what all that was? Other than what was pretty clear, I mean?"

"I can tell you more about it later, but yeah, you got the idea just from the one conversation." I wrap my arms around his neck. "You sure I can't just sit right there?" I point to the cushion next to him.

"Fine, I guess," he grumbles as T comes back in the room with one of my oversized wine glasses filled to the brim with a sweet, fruity wine.

I slide off his lap onto the couch, leaving absolutely no space between us.

Tansy points at me, then Liam. "Why get off his lap if you are gonna be that close anyway? Now catch me up."

CHAPTER 42

LIAM

"The only thing you missed was Azalea asking how my headache is today. I took the capsules you told me to take last night and this morning. I know there are still more ready in the kitchen, but I haven't needed more of them today."

"We think we have a little bit of an idea about it, but we aren't sure of the details," Hy adds. "We think that William is a former version of Liam. I don't really want to call it reincarnation, because it feels more like time and self are being manipulated. They aren't the same exact person, just in different times. They are different, but similar. I'm not explaining this very well." Hy gets flustered trying to explain.

"William has kept a lot of his memories separate from mine. It seems as if he shares what he feels I need to keep her safe. When he thought her safety was threatened yesterday, he forced himself forward, and instant migraine again."

· · ·

TANSY TAKES a sip of her wine and points at Z. "We skimmed through the journals. They are mostly just little things Mama didn't want to forget when we would do something sweet or silly."

Z nods and adds, "We didn't want to really read the ones where she was more serious because we know there are things there that we should read together. We were looking for specific things. Anything to do with the FateBond, and most of those are from just before she got pregnant with you and the first year after. We brought that one for you to read. It felt too intrusive to read it without you."

"Did you find anything else that could help?" *I'm really hoping they found something that will point us in the right direction at least.*

"Well, not exactly. I found a book in my stack of old lore, and I didn't even have time to tell T about it yet." Z looks up in apology at Tansy, "I haven't read it yet, but I brought it with me, along with the one for you, Hy."

Z GRABS HER OVERSIZED BAG, which she calls a purse, and brings a pretty purple notebook to Hy, but holds on to the old leather-bound book that looks as if it could fall apart at any moment.

"I know this isn't the same thing, but I...there's something in here that matters. I'm just not sure how or why." Z stumbles over the words like she isn't sure she wants to say them.

My head starts to pound as soon as Z stumbles over her words. "Okay, Azalea, you have my attention. What'd ye find, and why're ye afeared t' spit it out?"

Why? Why is William choosing now to assert himself? Hy isn't in danger. I have to figure out why he does this. This is all magic, who even knew that could be real? But there has to be something behind him being able to push me *aside to assert himself.*

. . .

THE ROOM GOES SILENT. Hyacinth moves back into my lap. "Liam?"

I drop my head onto her shoulder. "I'm ok, love. Just give me a minute." This is going to drive me crazy, if I'm not already. Who in their right mind speaks with a pirate accent? No one.

Z speaks slowly, as if she's afraid to make matters worse. "I think that shifters actually are real, not like werewolves or whatever from TV. But there are people who can shift into other things. This book hints at more than just myth. Maybe hidden truth?"

Now I know I'm dreaming. There is absolutely no way this is reality. The only good thing to come out of all this finding Hyacinth.

CHAPTER 43

HYACINTH

"Wait. What? You can't be serious right now."

"I am. It says something about. Wait, I have to find it again... Nytherical beings." Z points to the book.

Tansy gasps, "What did you just say?"

"Nytherical beings. It doesn't really say much, but I caught that. The print is difficult to read. I'm afraid I'm damaging the book as it is."

Tansy picks up her phone. "Nothing about them online. At least, that I can find," she shrugs.

Liam asks, "You did that on an incognito browser, right?"

"What? Did I do what now?" T asks him.

"Internet safety? You can't just go searching for things without protecting yourself." Mumbling, Liam goes on, "I thought I only had one woman to worry about. Good grief. This is going to be…"

He looks up, and we all three glare at him.

"What?" he asks.

"What? This is going to be what exactly?" I cross my arms and 'hmpf' at him.

"It's going to keep me on my toes, that's for sure." He pulls me back against him.

LIAM

"Did your mom ever mention what kind of magic gives you your gifts?"

The sisters shake their heads at me.

"Not even in her older journals? Did she have power?"

Tansy is the one to respond. "Her power had more to do with making things flourish and grow. The seeds she planted produced more fruit, and the crops were sturdier. She could also cultivate plants that don't usually thrive in Florida, though I don't know much about that part of it. I know some of the seeds she started for Tucker's parents—like the different varieties of tomatoes—still do really well. He uses the heirloom seeds and saves some every year because they perform best," she explains.

"You seem to know a lot about what Tucker does, T. Is there something we should know?" Z teases her.

"He explains things to me when he comes into the Garden. That's all. Stop giving him such a hard time. He's sweet," Tansy retorts.

"Sweet on you," Z comes back at her.

"He's too young for me, Z, be real. He's younger than you."

"What does that have to do with anything?" I ask her.

"It just. Argh! Let's get back to trying to figure out why

you're a pirate half the time." She empties her glass and waves a hand at Liam.

"WELL, Azalea, you said that book makes you think people can shift into something else? But then you said Nytherical beings. What brought you to the point of shifting?" I inquire, picturing the puzzle and all the pieces of information we have in my mind. Again, with all three women staring at me. "What? What did I do?"

"No wonder you were a captain in the Navy. You cut right through all the bullshit," Z says.

"I wasn't a captain in the Navy. I was an officer. I led missions because I could quickly and accurately read a situation and adapt. You're telling me that an answer is most likely in that book, but it has to do with people shifting into animals or some such shit. I want to know how that relates to a hitchhiking pirate in my brain."

Hyacinth leans over to hold my hand in both of hers. "I have an idea. Z, you said you didn't really get to go through the book in depth. Why don't the three of us go through Mama's journal while Liam goes through that one? We'll order takeout instead of cooking, so we should have some time to get a good start at least."

CHAPTER 44

HYACINTH

*L*iam is so tense beside me I'm afraid he's going to give himself another massive headache. "Is that okay with you? I didn't think you'd want to read all the mushy stuff about Mama and Rod. Come to think of it, I'm not sure I want to read all the mushy stuff either."

He gives me a small smile and kisses my forehead. *He does that a lot, and I absolutely love that he does.* "I'll switch to the chair so you can all sit together. Unless you'd rather move to the table?"

"Actually, Liam, if you don't mind, I'd appreciate it if you went to the table. Those pages aren't bound well in that book. If you're at the table, there's less chance of something being lost. I can give you a notepad for anything you find?" Z suggests.

After we are all settled in place, we open Mama's journal. Seeing her handwriting brings tears to my eyes. I know she's been gone ten years already, but I still miss her.

. . .

WE GO THROUGH DAILY chatty things. How much Tansy is growing, and how glad Mama is that the Garden is enough to provide for them. It's not surprising how often she mentions her Gram; she talked about her a lot. I get the feeling that keeping a journal was Mama's way of being able to still speak to Gram.

I turn the page scanning for anything that stands out as something that could be useful, when I come across a new passage.

"Look, here's something!" Tansy and Azalea both lean in closer to read.

November 20

I saw the most handsome man today. I'm sure it had something to do with him being in uniform. He stopped in to grab a small bouquet for his aunt, who he came to town to visit. I know I shouldn't be interested in anyone. I'm 19 with a six-month-old baby for crying out loud.

* * *

November 21

I can't stop thinking about that soldier. He came back into the shop! He wants to go to dinner, even though Tansy will have to come with us. He didn't care.

Oh my stars. He's my mate. He took my hand to lead me out the door, and I felt this energy flow up my arm. He didn't react, but he had Tansy's car seat, so what could he have done? He kept touching me all through dinner, though. He asked if he could see me again tomorrow.

* * *

November 22

Rod brought me lunch today from Hornebuckle's Bar. His aunt and uncle own it. He stayed with me and played with Tansy while I got all the Thanksgiving orders finished and ready for all the pick-ups. I'm closing as soon as they are all picked up so that we can spend more time together. He's taking me to dinner again. I love that he doesn't walk past me without touching me.

He asked me to go to his family's Thanksgiving dinner. He doesn't understand the pull he feels toward me, and I don't know what to tell him. Knowing that he's leaving in 2 days makes it hard for me to tell him about the FateBond. I know he'd believe me, but I don't want to add to his burden when he leaves. It will be hard enough just being away from each other. Mates don't separate for long periods of time after they complete the bond.

* * *

November 23

Happy Thanksgiving and Happy Birthday to me

Rod's family loved fawning all over Tansy. I don't think she was put down except for when she napped. His aunt Vera would have held her even then if she could.

Rod came back to the Garden with me. It's his last night before he goes back to his unit.

He asked if he could stay. I told him he would be my birthday gift to myself.

* * *

November 24

Rod gave me quite a few birthday gifts last night. Whew. Making love is so very different knowing he's my mate.

I accepted him. I know I shouldn't have. He doesn't even know anything about the Fate-Bond or being mates. But no one will ever be for me the way he is.

He doesn't know; he was asleep when I did it. But I bound myself to him. I will belong to no one else, and I'm okay with that.

Rod didn't want to leave me this morning. He asked if I would wait for him. That he knows I am it for him, and that he will come back to me, if I'll let him.

Of course, I told him I would gladly wait for him. I gave him Grandfather's watch. I have no gift that I could give that would be worth more than that. It is my biggest treasure, my last gift from my Grams. And it became my mate-gift, even though he doesn't know.

He won't tell me where he's going. He doesn't want me to worry. He said he'll write when he can, and he'll be home to me as soon as he can. He isn't planning to re-enlist. His uncle asked him to join him here in running the bar.

CHAPTER 45

HYACINTH

"I don't understand. How could he? This doesn't make sense." Hot tears streak down my cheeks before I even realize I'm crying, the confusion leaving a dull ache in my chest.

Tansy puts her arms around me and nods to Z, who brings Liam back into the living room.

Liam drops to his knees in front of me, his face full of concern. He gently brushes away my tears, voice soft. "What'd ye find, lass?"

"I don't even know what I found. But Mama found her mate, bound herself to him, and let him go." My voice trembles between anger and heartbreak. "I don't understand. How and why? We might find more answers in her journals, but why didn't he come back to her?"

Tansy and Z quietly move into the kitchen so that Liam and I can have a few moments alone.

. . .

"How could he do that? Do you feel the bond?"

"Listen, love, we don't know what else happened. The military wouldn't just let him stay. We can ask him about it when we—"

I cut Liam off. "Answer my question, Liam. Do you feel the bond? Because nothing in me believes you could walk away from me right now. Could you?"

"I don't know if I could walk away from you now, or tomorrow, or even next year. I feel tied to you, and I can't tell if it's the bond, or fate, or just us. But I know this: I don't want to walk away. I'm not poetic. I can't tell you fancy words or anything like that. What I can tell you is that I have been drawn to you since the first moment I saw you. Since you woke up, my life has been chaos. I wouldn't trade that chaos for stillness if it meant losing you. I will choose you in every lifetime that fate gives us. You have my heart until my last breath, and even after. I accept you and your FateBond and claim you as my own. If you want me." He leans his forehead against mine, the warmth of his breath grounding me.

"Please, love, accept me as your FateBond, willingly. Not because of some mystical pull, but because you chose me over any other man that fate could present as your choice," he whispers to me.

"I will choose you as my FateBond if you want me. I would accept you in any time that our paths could cross and choose you in every lifetime that fate would offer."

Liam wraps his arms around me and softly kisses me. My sisters come running into the room. "What did you do?"

"What? What did we do? Liam calmed me down?"

"You did something. I felt like the pressure of a storm releasing." Tansy tells us.

"No, it was like a breath of fresh air blew through the room," Azalea says.

"What did you feel, Hy?" Liam asks. "Because it sounds like your gifts showed themselves."

"I just felt relief that you accept me as I am, and want to be with me."

Tansy stutters, "Wh-what did you just say?"

"I'm relieved that he wants me as I am? That he wants to be with me? Why is that surprising, T?"

"Mama's journal. She said she accepted him as her Fate-Bond. She sealed it when she gave him her Grandfather's watch." Azalea points out.

CHAPTER 46

LIAM

"**S**o that's it to seal the FateBond? Accept each other and give each other a gift?" I can't believe it could be so simple.

Hyacinth shrugs her shoulders. "Let's look again."

"Mama said that she accepted him, and then she 'gave him Grandfather's watch.' She goes on to say 'It was her greatest treasure', so it became her mate-gift." Tansy paraphrases.

"Y'all really want to do this now? Now? You're going to seal the deal, stronger than a marriage? Now? We don't even know what all of this means." Azalea all but yells at us.

"Can we have a few more minutes, please? Would y'all go ahead and grab dinner? I just need a little time to talk to Liam," Hy asks her sisters.

"Fine." Z throws her hands up in the air and grabs her bag. "Coming, T?"

Tansy gives me a hard look before turning to follow Azalea out the door.

"Liam, I," Hyacinth says at the same time I say, "Listen, Hy—".

"Ladies first, please."

"You weren't calling me a lady earlier today." She says with a slight smile. "Go ahead. You can talk first."

"Okay." I stop to gather my thoughts. "I don't want you to feel pressured to do anything. Not because your sisters don't want you to do something, or because you think I want you to do something. I just want you to do what you want. I feel the pull between you and me. I think with time it will get stronger, and I'm pretty sure it's unbreakable already. I don't want to walk away from you. But I will. If you ask it of me, I will. That will be the only way I leave your side."

Tears stream down Hy's face. "I don't want you to walk away. I want to take this chance on us. But really, it's not even a risk. I feel you, like there's an invisible thread tying my heart to yours. When you're near, it's like I can finally breathe. I don't want to lose our chance at a one-in-a-million love, not for anything."

"Do you want to wait and finish the acceptance thing when your sisters are here or ten years from now, or do you want to finish it now? And that's if we are even doing it correctly?"

"Who knows? We don't have a manual or anything. All I know is that Mama's gift was her most valued possession."

"Wait here for a minute. I'll be right back." With a quick brush of my lips across her forehead, I go down the hall to our room. I open my bag and go to the hidden inner pocket and feel around for it. *There it is. Perfect.*

WALKING BACK into the family room, where Hyacinth is still standing in the same place, watching me. Neither of us speaks as I walk toward her. My heart is pounding as I hope she'll like the gift I chose for her.

I step in front of her, and unable to resist, kiss her quickly. "Hyacinth, I accept you as my FateBond, to be my true mate, and whatever else makes you mine. Please accept my gift. The only thing that made my life feel like it was worth anything until you." I place my dog tags over her head for her to wear until we can decide what she wants to do with them.

She clutches them, tears flowing freely. I pull her close, panic flickering. "Shhh, love. Did I do something wrong?"

She reaches up to grab my face. "You gorgeous, wonderful man. I accept you as my FateBond, to be my true everything," she laughs. "And whatever else will make you mine."

She takes her necklace off that I had found in the back room of the bar and loops the chain around my wrist. "Please accept my gift. The last gift my Mama gave me before she died."

Wrapping my arms around the most beautiful woman in the world, I fold her into my arms and kiss her as if I were a dying man, and she were the very air I breathe.

CHAPTER 47

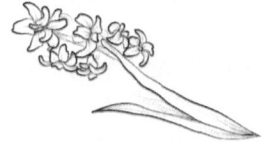

HYACINTH

"*W*hat are you thinking so hard about there, love?" Liam asks while nuzzling my throat.

What I'm actually thinking is, I need to see how much longer my sisters will be gone.

"I don't actually know if we did this whole accepting the bond thing correctly, but it certainly feels right. It almost seems as if I can sense you even more than before. Which is kind of an odd sensation."

He laughs in my ear. "That's not what you were thinking, but since I think your sisters should be back soon, I'll let you get away with it."

"And just how do you know what I'm thinking, Captain?"

"Because I'm thinking it too. And I bet I can take care of you at least once before they get back here."

Raising an eyebrow at this playful side of him, "I don't think so. They could walk in on us."

"Not if," he says, pulling me into the bedroom and closing the door behind me. "I bring you in here."

PUSHING me backward on the bed, he doesn't even remove my panties before he's diving in. He just moves them to the side out of his way.

"You should wear nothing but dresses for the remainder of our days, love."

"That's not very practical, Captain."

"C'MON, love. Give me one before yer sisters get back here."

"Mmmm, I think I'm going to make you work for this one."

Ripping my panties, he attacks with teeth and fingers until I'm screaming his name. *"Make me work for it and I'll confiscate all your panties."*

"You will not take my panties away, you pirate!" I laugh at him.

"What?" Wiping his mouth and helping me up, he looks at me quizzically. "What did you say?"

"I said you can't take all my panties. You said you were going to confiscate them."

"Hy, I didn't say that. I thought it, but I didn't say it."

"Of course you did. I heard you."

MY SISTERS ARE COMING BACK in with dinner. *I really wish they had been just a few more minutes so that we could finish talking.*

"I'm pretty sure we were done talking, Wench." Liam leers at me.

"Ummm, Liam? I didn't say anything."

LIAM

I walk out to greet her sisters while Hyacinth cleans up a bit. I'm not even a bit sorry for taking those few minutes to pleasure her. I have an idea that we are about to upset both Tansy and Azalea.

"Where's Hy?" Z asks, and T looks at me like she knows what I was just doing.

I don't really mind if they know what I was doing. I intend to make their sister happy, both in bed and out of it.

"She went to the bathroom. She'll be out in a minute."

I WANT to test this thing of hearing each other's thoughts. I concentrate on Hy while her sisters set out all the food, and I have a seat at the table to stay out of their way.

I think about how much I love her curves and how soft her skin is. I think about how she sounds when she screams my name, and I love it. Shit, I'm thinking about how much I already love her. And now I'm sitting here, hard, and trying to backpedal my thoughts so I won't embarrass myself.

Hy slips her arms around my neck from behind and whispers in my ear, "Love you too, Captain. Remember, two can play this game."

"*Do we let your sisters know about this new development?*" I think at her.

She gives me a quick shake of her head.

"Okay. You two are being super weird. Why?" Tansy demands.

"He ravished me right before y'all got back, and you almost caught us." Hy blurts out.

I cover my smile with my hand. "Why don't I just go… somewhere…to the bathroom, or something?" I'm trying so hard not to laugh at their expressions.

"*Well, it worked, didn't it?*" Her smug voice echoes inside my head.

I MIGHT BE JUSTIFIABLY LOSING my mind with two...wait. I don't have William's pulsing pressure in my head. I'm not sure whether this is good or bad.

I hear a dish drop, and Hyacinth comes rushing into the living room, where I stop when I realize I don't have two extra voices.

"What's wrong?" she demands, with her sisters hot on her heels.

"I don't think William is trying to beat my head in anymore."

"I wondered if this would happen if you started the bonding. My guess is you two," Z points back and forth between us, "accepting who you are to each other, cemented where William and Liam should be. Kind of the heart forcing the mind to accept. I'm really interested to see what happens once you complete the bond."

I REACH out to snag Hy's hand as we walk back to the kitchen for dinner. "I'm sorry I made you lose him," I whisper to her.

She spins around and runs into me to make me stop where I am. "You listen to me, and you listen good. Liam, I choose you. I accept you. I will remind you every damn day if I have to. You didn't make me lose him. He is a part of you. Most importantly, he gave me you. I will cherish you all the more for his sacrifice." With her finger poking me in the chest, accentuating every word she says, "You are mine. You. Do you understand me?"

Grabbing the finger she was poking me with I pull her against me. "Understood, love."

CHAPTER 48

HYACINTH

I can't believe I just went off on Liam. This is surreal. Two days ago, I wouldn't let him go because I felt William when Liam touched me. Now I sense Liam and our bond. I wish I understood how the bond could have started with William, but then really have belonged to Liam.

We all fix our plates in the kitchen to take to the table. I swear, my sisters must have ordered everything on the menu, and a double order of crab rangoon.

Everyone seems lost in thought while we eat, until Tansy observes, "Hyacinth, what did you do?"

I stop with the fork halfway to my mouth and set it back down. "What do you mean?"

She points with her fork at Liam's wrist. "That's your necklace."

Uh oh. I should've known I couldn't keep it from them for even just a day. I feel Liam's warmth through our bond. Will this ever feel normal? *"God, I hope not,"* he says through our bond.

"It's my gift to him." I pull his dog tags out from inside my dress. "And this is his to me. Our most prized possessions, given freely to each other."

Z looks like she's watching a tennis match with her head bouncing back and forth between me and Tansy.

"Why didn't you just tell us?" T demands, obviously hurt.

Liam soothes, "It's new. Two days ago, I didn't know you. I had only seen Hyacinth for the first time the day she passed out to go meet another version of me. We have had all of one morning alone to—"

Z covers her ears. "I don't really want to hear what y'all did when you were alone!"

Her silliness breaks the tension in the room.

"Look, this is new. We don't know what it all means, except that we have accepted each other and are bound," I say. "We have no idea how that will affect us, or whether the initial effects will taper off. Goodness, there may even be more things that pop up!" I throw my hands up in the air. "Who knows what will happen next?"

Azalea gets that look in her eye. The one that tells us something is brewing in her brilliant mind. "What initial effects?"

Liam's eyes snap to mine, and I feel him questioning what I want to do. He answers her honestly. "We can feel each other's thoughts and emotions. Shit, I'm pretty sure we're straight-up telepathic with each other."

LIAM

"Wait, wait, wait a minute." Z is clearly piecing together a puzzle in her mind. "You went from having William forcing thoughts and memories, to being able to speak to Hy telepathically?"

"Wow. Oh wow. Oh wow, oh wow. I think I've got it. Liam, give me Hy's necklace. Hy, give me Liam's dog tags." Azalea is serious.

Hy reaches up and grabs hold of my tags, wrapping both hands around them. "No. You can't have them."

Z holds her hands out to each of us in expectation.

"The lass said, 'No.' Ye'll not be takin' her chain, and that be the end of it."

With a huge smile, Z looks me dead in the eye. "How's the headache?"

Hy's concern trickles through our bond, so I try to send her loving, I'm okay vibes. "I don't have a headache, Z. Why do you want Hy's necklace?"

"Oh, I don't. What I wanted was for you to feel like something important was affecting Hy, and for her to be upset by it. I wanted to see if William would lash out and try to protect her. What I think, and keep in mind that it's all conjecture, is that William needed to know you would protect her like he did. I don't know how long you'll talk like a pirate when you feel like she's threatened or upset. It may be the territorial part of the equation has sort of melded together. I don't know the how or why, but I will continue searching to find out more." Azalea leans back and crosses her arms with a satisfied smile.

HY LOOKS AT ME, then back to Z. "Does this have anything to

do with you making sure the pain caps had something to do with acceptance?"

"Maybe? Liam had to accept his former self as part of himself. More than anything, it was just a feeling," Z replies.

Tansy leans forward on the table. "You know that after just two days together, you have committed for life, right? This is stronger than marriage; it's breakable only by death."

"I would say that's not completely true. Hyacinth and William found each other, but didn't complete the bond. Yet, even death didn't separate them. He followed her. Since I can feel her, I'm fairly certain she can still feel him."

"No," Hy says, and all eyes turn on her. I take her hand, fear and worry emanating off her. "I don't feel him anymore. I did at first, but little by little, you sort of blended into one. I only feel you."

Love pours through our bond. Has it really only been a week since I first laid eyes on this incredible woman?

"While everyone's together, I told Rod I'd go back to the bar tomorrow morning. I don't know exactly how we will work this out. I was working both shifts while Hy was in the hospital. I don't know what normal is there."

"You'll definitely have to work tomorrow night. It's ladies' night!" Z dances in her seat.

"I want to go up there tomorrow before the lunch rush. I need at least some answers from him." Hy looks at both her sisters. "Do either of you have an issue with me taking the journal with me?"

They both shake their heads and then clean up the dinner mess. "Who wants the leftovers?" I ask them.

"Acting like you own the place already." Z snickers. "I'll take them with me so we can have them for lunch tomorrow."

CHAPTER 49

HYACINTH

I get dressed to go to Horney's with Liam. I'm not sure if I'm more nervous or anxious about seeing Rod today. Liam sent him a text that we would be there around nine-thirty instead of ten.

At some point, someone had brought my car home. I'll have to remember to ask who it was so I can thank them. The rain falls in a constant drizzle today, making riding Liam's bike a challenge. His smile and emotions waft through the FateBond.

I'm pretty sure he liked me hanging on to him for dear life when we went for a ride yesterday.

"I'll take you hanging on to me anytime, anywhere, love. Ready?"

He holds his hand out for my car keys. "What if I want to drive?" I ask him.

"You don't." His answer is simple and true.

"Do we have a plan for this? What do you plan to say to Rod?" he asks.

"I honestly don't. I don't know how to act or what to say. I don't know why he walked away. I know he came back and stayed a part of my life, but I don't know why or how he could walk away from her."

IT'S NOT FAR to the bar, just a few minutes. The whole way, Liam has one hand on my thigh just under the hem of my skirt, full of concern.

"Before we go in, I want to say something, and I don't want you to misunderstand. I'm on your side. Always. Nowhere else for me to be. Rod was in the military, and he couldn't just stay with your mom. He had to report. I don't know what else happened, but I know that. He had to go. Remember that when you are talking to him. He may have had a reason beyond what anyone here knew."

He leans across and gives me a quick kiss before coming around to open my door. Even in the rain, I know better than to open the door and go in without waiting. It's the first time we've been anywhere, but I know he wants to do things like this for me. In some ways, our bond makes life a little easier. I suppose we'll find out how it doesn't as time goes on.

LIAM

It feels like it's been years instead of days since I was last here to work. A lot has happened since I rolled into this town a week ago. Holding the door for Hy, I immediately place my hand on the small of her back as we walk in. Rod is waiting for us at a booth toward the back.

I lean down to brush a kiss on the top of her head. "I'll go do inventory so you'll have a few minutes."

Rod looks like he hasn't slept in weeks. "Thanks."

She squeezes my hand as she sits down across from him at the table.

I stop at the station behind the bar where Rod keeps his inventory list, and head into the back room. The room looks so much like it did in the past, when I—I mean, when William—found Hyacinth. That memory feels like mine, not something forced on me. I shake my head at the odd sensation.

I REACH out to feel if Hy's okay. I'm not trying to eavesdrop on her thoughts or conversation; I just need to feel her presence. I don't know if I hope the constant need to feel her will settle down, or never go away, or remain forever.

She's holding it together, and sent a wave of love as soon as she felt my touch. *God, I love that woman.*

With nothing left to do for inventory, I go into the kitchen. Al isn't here yet, but I can at least get a head start on slicing the lemons and limes for the bar until Hy is finished talking to Rod.

CHAPTER 50

HYACINTH

Sitting across from Rod, I'm not really sure how to start our conversation. He looks rough and exhausted. He pulls out Mama's letter from his pocket and hands it over to me.

"I didn't mean to keep it. I can't say I'm sorry enough to—"

"Rod, stop. I'm not blaming—well, that's not true—I am blaming you, and I'm trying to let that go. We have a lot we need to discuss, but we can't change what's already done and over with. I'm mad. I'm really mad. At both you and Mama. She's not here to answer for her choices. You are, but I don't even know where to start."

He reaches down and adjusts his old ratty watch. I stare at it for a moment before I pick up Mama's journal I brought with me.

"I have an idea of where to start, but I don't know what you know. I guess we can start with this." I open the journal to the page where she met him all those years ago and spin it around for him to read.

He pulls it to him with a shaking hand, but has a small smile as he reads what she wrote.

"YOUR MOTHER WAS SO BEAUTIFUL. Azalea looks so much like her, sometimes I think I see her goin' past." He gently runs his finger down the page before he turns it. "Tansy was such a happy little thing, I loved playin' with her that day. I thought I'd adopt..." He stops speaking, closes his eyes and bows his head as he tries to catch his breath, lost in his memories.

Liam reaches out to check on me through our bond. I'm glad he did. I needed to feel him, just for a moment. I don't get how Rod could have stayed away if he felt even just a fraction of this. I send what I hope is a feeling of my love for him.

"Is that Mama's watch she gave you?" I finally ask.

He looks up at me with red-rimmed eyes, nodding. "I'm guessin' she wrote about that too."

I nod back. "Keep reading, there's not much more I need you to see."

Rod looks back down and turns the page again. I know the moment he sees what she did. He looks as if someone just punched him.

"I... I don't—Hy, I had to leave. I had to report. I don't know what this means." I reach across the table to gently close the book.

SHAKING HIS HEAD, he says, "I loved her, Hy. Hell, I love her still, and she's not even here."

Rod is honestly starting to scare me. I know he's not that

old, but he's trembling so hard and isn't breathing right. Before I have time to panic completely, Liam is beside me.

He quickly moves to kneel beside Rod. "Okay, old man, you're scaring Hy. Take a deep breath in and count with me, ready? Breathe in, one, two, three. Relax."

I grab onto Liam's hand and squeeze. "I mean, really, Rod. You're the one who taught me to breathe and count. We can do this, ready?"

After counting breaths just a few more times, he doesn't look like he is going to hyperventilate anymore.

LIAM

I slide into the booth next to Hyacinth and wrap my arm around her shoulders. She immediately leans into me.

Rod watches us closely. "Is this what she meant? How y'all are?"

We look at each other, then back at him. Hyacinth nods. "We think so, but since we don't know anyone else like me, we don't know for sure."

"ROD, there's one question that Hy really needs answered. Why didn't you come back to Meadow?"

"I did. She was with someone else. My whole team was brought home, and we weren't far away, just a couple of hours. I had a one-day pass, so I drove over. I was walkin' toward the Garden, and I saw some guy. I don't know who he was; I didn't stick around to find out. Anyway, I saw him kiss her, and when she turned, I could see she was pregnant, could only've been a couple of months, the baby bump wasn't big. So, I left without talkin' to her. If she was happy, I wasn't gonna mess that up. I drove back to the base."

"Oh, Rod. I'm so sorry. I don't know who it was you saw, I

don't. But Mama was very sick with me. She hardly gained any weight at all, and I was small. She was due in late August, but was so sick and had so much trouble, she had me early in July."

"Ah, hell, hon. I should've figured it out just from your birthday, but I didn't think too hard about it. I have no excuse. I can only hope you forgive me."

"Can we just take it a little slow? You've been so important to me for so long, I don't want to lose that, but there's still a lot for us to work through."

"I'll be here anytime you need me. That won't change. I'll give you the space if that's what you want, Hy."

Hyacinth is something else. I know how torn up she is, and that she needs to understand more about what happened. She's trying to move forward and wrap her mind around the whole situation. Not only did she suddenly gain a mate, but a father.

CHAPTER 51

HYACINTH

So much change, all in a week. I don't know how to process all of this. I don't want to lose Rod, so I have to come to terms with the situation. I'm sure there will be a lot more of the heavy talks in the next few weeks and months.

Al comes walking in to prepare for lunch, ending our discussion.

"I need to follow up with Doc to make the new fancy doctor that Z can't stand happy. You'll be okay here, since we rode in together?" I ask Liam.

"Of course. You know I'll be here until midnight or later helping with ladies' night. I guess we'll find out how we handle being away from each other."

Liam slides out of the booth so I can get up. Rod's still sitting there as I stand to leave. I reach up to kiss Liam, silently telling him, *"Guess we'll see how far we can be away from each other and still communicate, too."*

I reach down and place my hand on Rod's shoulder. "We'll get there, Rod."

Liam hands over my keys as I pick up my phone to text my sisters' group chat.

> Me: Heading into town to see Doc. Just a follow up, nothing to worry about

As I get into the car, T responds with Z right after.

> T: One of us should go with you anyway

> Z: I volunteer as tribute

Why would she want to go? She can't stand that new doctor. After buckling my seat belt I respond.

> Me: really? Why?

My phone dings with a response before I can even put the care in reverse.

> Z: just come get me

> Me: on my way

LIAM

Damn. Watching her leave was harder than I expected it to be. She's just going into town, and that's all. Rod asks if I'm alright. I jerk my head in what I hope is a positive response. My head is pounding.

"I'm here." I feel her words brush across my mind, and the tension eases. *"Call me when you stop."* I think to her, and hope it makes sense.

My phone rings immediately. "You haven't stopped yet."

"I have CarPlay. What's wrong?"

"Nothing. It's okay now. My head started hurting as soon as you left. I can't help but think William had something to do with it, but as soon as I felt you, it eased. I don't know. This will take getting used to, I guess. And finding out how far this telepathy thing goes."

"I'm at The Garden, I'll see if Z has any of the capsules I can bring you. She wanted to go with me to see Doc."

"I don't need them now. Let me know when you get there. I can't believe I'm the sap saying this, but it's true. I miss you already. Drive safe."

"I love you, Captain."

"WELL, now, that certainly didn't take long." Tucker says. I turn as he comes in the back with today's delivery.

"What didn't take long?" I ask him, perplexed.

"You two mating up. It didn't take long. I overheard Tansy and Z talking about you staying at Hy's. I figured that's what was going on," he explained.

I nod, and then I realize what he said. "Wait a minute. What do you know about the mate bond?"

"I know they are Nytherica. Most of the women are some form of witches, and I assume all three of them are as well. I know Tansy controls the weather, but she doesn't know that I know, so please don't let on. I don't know if she...I don't know how this will turn out for me yet."

I snap my jaw closed when I realize I'm gaping at him. How does he know so much? "Tucker, the girls need to talk to you. They have been isolated from it all; there's so much they don't know. We don't even know if we got the bonding stuff right. It just kind of happened." I tell him.

"I'll be glad to help if I can, but it's not like I know much beyond my kin. I need to tell Tansy in my own time and talk to her about…"

My eyes widen, and I rub the back of my neck. "Well, that might be a small problem. Hy probably knows everything I know." *I can feel her reaching for me as if she's worried I'll get another headache.*

Tucker sighs and pinches the bridge of his nose. "Mates, you have to share everything. Look, just give me a day or so to talk to Tansy, please."

I can't tell if he's asking me or Hy—or both.

Customers come in for lunch, so Rod calls out to let us know.

"No, you aren't understanding me. Hy knows what I know because of the bond. She knows everything I know."

Tucker's jaw drops. "Okay then. I'll be back after I make the rest of my deliveries. Maybe we can talk then."

CHAPTER 52

HYACINTH

I have Z drive me to town to see Doc. It's a little disorienting to have the bond bouncing in my brain, pulling my attention away from everything else. I keep feeling like I need to check in with Liam. It won't be healthy for either of us to be so very needy all the time.

I keep reaching out, and I feel him doing the same. I don't know if either of us are doing it intentionally. I know he's with Tucker, but it's confusing because Z is talking at the same time.

I feel him again. This time it's intentional. *"Love, I don't know if you got any of that, but I need you to keep it to yourself until we can talk. I'm guessing you can still understand me, though I can sense how confused you are. Try to focus on Z. It should help."*

I turn my attention to Z and what she's talking about. "And I think I'm going to have to tell him just to leave her alone since she won't do it."

"What? I zoned out. You want to tell who to leave who alone?"

With a sigh, Azalea repeats, "Tucker. He won't leave T alone. She won't speak up, so I will."

"Z, you will not. You need to leave them alone. If she didn't want him to keep coming around, she would put a stop to it."

She pulls into the parking lot at Dr. Harley's office and turns my car off. "I'm coming in with you."

Doc typically sees us close to lunchtime after someone overheard part of a conversation with Mama. Today, though, my appointment is earlier. We walk in, and Dr. Reyes is talking with Doc.

Dr. Reyes steps forward, hand outstretched to me. I look at Doc in confusion, but shake Dr. Reyes' hand. "I hope you don't mind. I asked Dr. Harley to allow me to stop by for your appointment this morning. He cleared his schedule for the hour."

Z huffs and crosses her arms. "Well, we do mind, thank you very much."

Dr. Reyes turns and extends his hand out to her. "I would very much like to start over again, if I may."

Z hesitates, but shakes his hand.

"I apologize sincerely for my behavior the day we met. I have no adequate excuse. I humbly beg your forgiveness." He finally releases Z's hand.

I'm in awe. He rendered my sister speechless.

"Shall we go to my office?" Dr. Harley offers.

After we all sit, I say, "Doc, I'm fine, really. I was tired the first day I went home, but I'm good."

Dr. Reyes asks, "Could you tell me what happens when you do this? I've never seen or heard of anything like it. Dr. Harley said you usually just faint. There are tests we can run to determine the cause."

"As I've told Dr. Harley, anytime we've run tests, nothing has come back. I'm not willing to be a pincushion when it's always been inconclusive." My tone gets defensive, and Liam jumps to the front of my mind filled with concern.

"But there are…"

"Dr. Reyes, I'm not doing the testing. I'm not changing my mind."

He leans back in his chair. "I had to at least try. Dr. Harley told me you wouldn't consider it."

"Dr. Harley was correct," I state.

WE ALL STAND TO LEAVE, but I wait for Z and Dr. Reyes to walk before I whisper to Doc that I need birth control.

He clears his throat. "I have one more question for Hyacinth before y'all leave. She'll be out in a minute."

LIAM

The longer Hyacinth is away, the more restless I feel. I know she's on her way back, but not understanding how this bond works is stressful. I keep checking to make sure she's okay and not overwhelmed.

Rod comes out of the back office, so I ask, "I'm going to need to leave for a bit after lunch to help the girls with a few things. I'll make sure I'm back by 4:00 to help get ready for tonight, if that's okay with you?"

"Yep, been handling this place for years."

. . .

I WALK OUT JUST as she pulls up in front. Opening her door, I hold out a hand to help her out. "You know I can get out of a car myself, right?"

"Of course you can," I tell her, wrapping my arms around her and resting my chin on her forehead. "We're going home, then coming back at four."

I walk her around the car and get her settled, feeling her laughter through our bond, but not caring if it's a little much. Handing her my phone, I ask, "Can you text Tucker to meet us at the house?"

"You have Tucker's number already? I don't even have his number."

"Got it when Rod was running back and forth to the hospital. How much of our conversation were you able to pick up on?"

"I don't actually hear everything you hear. Do you...hear everything I do?"

"More like I get the impression and your feelings. I know if you're happy or frustrated unless you think directly at me, I guess."

CHAPTER 53

LIAM

*T*ucker pulls up just after we get back to the house. After getting drinks for everyone, we settle at the table.

"Tucker, can you explain what you were telling me this morning?"

Tucker sighs, "I don't really know what to say. My kin has been here for generations. There's a lot of history that is specific to each kin, so things could be different for y'all."

Hy asks, "So, you can't tell us anything about how the bond works or the accepting thing?"

HE RUNS his hand down his face slowly. "I can try, but will you tell me your power? I'm guessing telepathy since Liam said you would know what he knows?"

"That only happened when we accepted and bonded, I think?" I look over at Hy to make certain I'm correct.

She nods. "Well, there were a few other times when it felt like you were answering things that I didn't think I said out loud, but nothing like this until after."

"Then what's your gift, Hyacinth?" Tucker asks.

Holding onto her hand, I answer him. "She time travels."

"What?" He puts his head in his hands and starts laughing. "Y'all are joking. No one has time-traveled in centuries that we know of."

We look at him and wait. "Oh, shit—Pardon, me, Hyacinth. Excuse my language, please. You aren't kidding."

"CAN you tell us anything about how the bond is supposed to work?"

He shakes his head. "Even different families within a kin can have different traditions for it. There's usually a wedding ceremony, and then the couple will have a much smaller ceremony for the mating. Sometimes, the immediate family will come to that, but no one else, and most people prefer to be alone for it. The family's traditional words are spoken. I don't know what y'all's would be.

Afterward, a gift is given. The gift is a bigger deal than you might think. It needs to be something tangible and significant that you can see and hold on to. Most people won't even let others know what the gift is. Some of the old folks believe that if the mating gift is removed, then the bond is too. It's not true, though. That's a story for another time."

Hy eagerly asks, "So if we say our family's traditional words and exchange a meaningful gift, we are actually mated? Is that why the telepathy thing happened?"

"I would say yes, you are definitely mated. I don't know about the telepathy. Why don't I call my Gramma? I don't know that most people in my kin even know y'all are Nytheric, but she will keep it to herself if we ask her to."

"I know you asked Liam not to tell Tansy, but Tucker, this is the first time we have found other people that might be like us. I need to talk to her about this."

"Please just give me one day to talk to her first," he begs.

HYACINTH

"I don't know if we should call your grandmother without Tansy and Azalea, but we need to at least know what's going on with us," Liam agrees, so Tucker calls her.

"Hey, Gramma. I have some friends that have some questions about the FateBond. Do you have a few minutes to talk with us?"

He puts his phone down on the table, and the screen lights up. "Okay, Gramma, I have you on speakerphone now so they can talk to you."

"Um, hi?"

"Hello, ma'am." Liam says, leaning forward.

"Well, don't y'all sound cute. Y'all have some questions about the FateBond? Most kin teach their own, but I'll try to help if I can." Her voice is sweet and scratchy, like I would imagine Mama's Grams would have sounded.

"My mom was the only one I know of who would know, and she died more than 10 years ago. I never had the opportunity to learn any of it from her."

"Oh, well, now, honey, I'm sure sorry to hear that. You touched your mate and found him, did ya?"

LIAM CHUCKLES as I answer her. "Well, I went back in time and met my pirate mate, then came back to our time, and found my Liam."

"Oh, dear. Did you just say...you're a traveler? We haven't

had a traveler in several generations now. We thought y'all had all but faded."

Liam sits straighter in his chair. "Can you tell us anything about Hy's gift then, ma'am?"

"Oh, I can tell you what the stories said, but there's not much known. A traveler will travel until she finds her mate. There's all kinds of stories about having to find him in the past in order to find him in the present. And once she finds him, she can't travel anymore. She can hear his thoughts instead."

"That's what happened! I found William in the past, but as soon as I came home I found Liam, and we can hear each other's thoughts and talk to each other like a mind meld. I didn't know I wouldn't travel again. Do you know why?"

I WAS SO excited to hear about my gift, I was practically bouncing in my chair.

"Well, now then, dear, it wouldn't be a good idea to time-travel if there were a baby involved, now would it?"

I blush so hard I feel like a tomato. "Can you tell us anything about Liam having William's memories?"

"Oh my. There was a story about a princess traveler who found her mate, and he was killed while she was with him. He actually died saving her. Now, mind you, I heard this story when I was a teenager."

She chuckled and paused before going on with her tale. "Anyway, the story said that his spirit came forward with her to continue to keep her safe. She found her mate right quick, but he had a real hard time with the memories and such that came from her knight."

"You mean this will be permanent? Him pushing his thoughts forward on me?" Liam asked.

"I don't know what happened to them. I thought it was a

pretty fairytale. It would only make sense that it would settle down. Any old tales of a true love sacrificing himself for his mate, it's always a protective spirit that lingers."

"GRAMMA, wasn't there a story about two people's memories? It wasn't a traveler, but something happened to her first FateBond mate?" Tucker asks, speaking for the first time since we started the call.

"Oh! I forgot about them! Yes! Once her original mate was sure of her safety and happiness, his memories just settled into the new mate. Now that was a bit different because it took time for her to grieve. I can only imagine that the memories would be a little more traumatic if it were instant, like for a traveler. But they did settle in."

"Ma'am, we really appreciate you taking the time to talk to us today. Thank you." Liam tells her.

"Well, sugar, I can talk all day. Y'all have Tucker bring y'all 'round to visit me. I'd sure love to meet ya both."

"Yes, ma'am, we'll try," I tell her with a laugh.

As Tucker leaves, he tells us she will expect to meet us soon, so we should plan on it.

LIAM STUTTERS A BIT. "SO, UM, BABY?"

"I don't think she meant literally right now. I got the shot when I was visiting Doc today. We can talk and make decisions later, but I don't want the concern right now."

CHAPTER 54

HYACINTH

*L*iam asks, "What are your plans for tonight while I'm at the bar?"

"We usually have dinner together on Thursday nights at Horney's, so I guess I need to check in and make sure we're still planning for that. Since T should have Hawthorne tonight, we may need to make different plans."

> Me: dinner at Horney's?

It doesn't take long before both of my sisters respond to my text.

> Z: hell yeah!

> T: Asshole's keeping Thorny again, sure

I get in the car before I reply to them.

> Me: headed there now

> Z: watchin your man 😒

Smiling to myself, I reply.

> Me: yup 😊

By the time I'm finished texting, we are back at Horney's. Rod looks twice when we walk in. I guess he wasn't expecting me back today.

"We always eat here on Thursdays," I remind him.

"Didn't know if you would today." He wipes down the already clean bar top.

"Rod, we'll be okay," I tell him.

I REACH up to grab a quick kiss from Liam before I tell them, "I'm going to help Al for a while."

Rod asks Liam if I'm okay as I walk away. "She will be. Give her time. I don't think she wants space, just time to adjust," my mate tells him.

I send him a wave of love with, *"Thank you. That was perfect."*

AL LOOKS up as I walk in and opens his arms for a hug. "Aren't you a sight for sore eyes?"

I lean into the hug for a moment and feel a disgruntled rumble through our bond.

"You can't be jealous."

In return, *"I can. He's still a man, love."*

"How can I help, Al? The girls won't be here for at least an hour. Put me to work."

"Would you mind rolling out some of the pizza dough for me? It's doing well since you conned Rod into putting it on the ladies' night menu."

We work quietly together until Liam sneaks up behind me, wrapping me in a hug. "Your sisters are here, love."

"You could have just—"

He interrupts me. "Then I wouldn't have gotten to do this." He kisses my neck and spins me around.

Al grunts, "Outta my kitchen with that. Crazy kids smoochin' up in my kitchen. What's this place turnin' into?"

I GET to the table to see Tansy and Z both with their regular drinks, but there's not one waiting for me. I start to go up to the bar when Liam comes to the table. "Okay, ladies, I know it's ladies' night and all. I also know that you all three had a little too much last week, so I'm trying something special out for you tonight. Each of you has your very own nonalcoholic versions of your usuals."

We each raise an eyebrow at him.

"Now, I'm not one to typically tell someone not to drink, but I'd appreciate it if y'all would at least give these a try for me. On your next round, just let me know if you'd like leaded instead of unleaded. Fair enough?"

While he's with us, Gary and Erika come in and head straight for our table again. Z introduces Liam as my man, and he and Gary shake hands. They head off to find their own table, already talking about what they want to order tonight. Before Liam can walk away, a few more people stopped by to meet him. Word is spreading fast that I'm off the market.

The three of us have our usual Thursday night fun, laughing and chatting with our friends that come in. Tucker is hanging out at the bar talking to Liam.

Every time I look up to watch Liam, he sends me a smile. If he's watching me so much, I don't quite know how he's getting much done.

Z GOES up to the bar to get a "leaded" margarita; T and I decide to go with her to let someone else have our table. Once we grab seats, T tells me, "I think I'm going to head home. I'm ready to call it a night."

I know it's still early, but I don't question her.

Z grabs her margarita and flits around the tables, chatting up all our friends. I'm perfectly content watching my captain behind the bar.

"I'm not a captain. I keep telling you." He laughingly sends to me.

He and Rod are a good team. If I didn't know differently, I would think they'd worked together for years. One will mix drinks while the other helps tables and seamlessly switch off.

"HEY, BARTENDER," I call out to Liam when he slows down. "I'd like another rum runner, please. Are you sure they are nonalcoholic? I don't feel tipsy or anything, but I wouldn't have known if you hadn't told me."

"I looked up different ways to make nonalcoholic drinks. Rum runner was honestly one of the more difficult ones to figure out since we don't have nonalcoholic rum. Al helped, and we came up with this version. I thought you might like it, and after last week's revelry, I thought all of you ladies would like something zero-proof tonight."

"It's really good. Maybe we should talk to Rod about offering a few different ones on a regular basis."

Once things finally slow down, Rod tells Liam, "Take our girl on home." And I'm truly glad he did. I'm tired.

LIAM

It only takes a few minutes for us to get home. Wow. It hits me.

I don't think I've ever truly felt this way. Foster home to foster home, then base to base or on sea duty in the Navy. Roaming for the last year, having this feeling of searching, but not knowing what I was searching for. It all led me to this.

To her.

As soon as we get inside, Hyacinth turns and wraps her arms around me, holding tight. "I would ask what's wrong, but since I can feel what you're feeling, I know it's not that something's wrong. What is it?"

I shake my head slightly. "I don't know if I can explain it very well. We pulled into the driveway, and then it hit me. I'm home. After roaming and searching, I finally found what I had been searching for. I'm home. You. You are my home."

EPILOGUE

TUCKER

I can't believe Tansy doesn't know there are other Nytherical people nearby. Much less that I am too. I've waited patiently, trying to build trust, but she must feel it too.

I've run out of time since Liam and Hy want me to talk to my kin.

She looks amazing tonight in fitted jeans that show every curve and accentuate her long legs. The flowy things she's wearing over her tank top keeps shifting and showing just enough cleavage to drive me wild.

SHE'S SAYING goodbye to her sisters, so I guess it's now or never. I catch her as she nears the door.

"Tansy, wait."

· · ·

SHE MOVES to the side of the room with me. "Tucker, I... yeah?"

"I know you feel this, Tansy. I'm just asking for a chance. Please." I'll beg her if I have to.

"Tucker, I... can't. I can't do this." She's shaking her head, clearly torn, but still refusing.

"So, you're rejecting me then? That's it. Not even a chance?" I can't believe this. Not really.

SHE STANDS THERE, stunning and silent, shaking her head slowly. I turn to leave, but lightning strikes nearby just before I reach the door.

I turn around and march back to her. I know I shouldn't say anything when I'm angry and hurt, but I can't help myself.

"So what? You don't want me, but you don't want me to leave? I know that was you, Tansy. I know you, probably better than you think."

I TURN AROUND and take a step toward the door before she can even reply.

Spinning back, I grab her and kiss her with every pent-up emotion I have. I pour everything into that single kiss since it may be the only one I ever get.

"THINK ABOUT THAT, Tansy. Think about what we can be if you'll just take a chance."

THEN I TURN and walk out the door.

WANT MORE?

Well, I sure hope you enjoyed spendin' time with Hyacinth and Liam as much as I did writin' their story.

If you're cravin' some of the goodies from their kitchen (and maybe a sip or two of those drinks), you can find some of the recipes in the Southern Sisters Cookbook.

Now don't you worry, Tansy and Azalea have stories of their own comin' in 2026, and they've got plenty to say.

If you'd like to be the first to know when they're ready, come on and join my newsletter Humid Nights and Hot Reads. I'd love to keep in touch, darlin'.

You can find me at www.TCLynndale.com.

ACKNOWLEDGMENTS

Y'all, this book wouldn't have made it to the end without my people. I need to thank a few of them.

First of all, my amazing hubby. Thank you for sacrificing TV time for writing time, and always supporting me no matter what dream I decide to chase.

I have to thank my mom for inspiring an incredible love of reading. You gave me the gift of story, and that's what led me here. I hope I've made you proud.

I have two amazing mentors, and I can't thank either of them enough for encouraging me to finish this. Erin and Lacy, y'all are the compass that keeps me from spinning in circles!

My admin team is the best! Kellie, Heather, Hilary, Priscilla, Tabi, and Trista, y'all are so fun to hang out with online. Bless y'all for listenin' to me ramble, dream, and sometimes plain ol' panic about what to do and how to do it. Y'all are the best kind of sounding board.

My Porch Posse's excitement, encouragement, and way of shoutin' about my stories louder than I ever could... y'all are pure magic.

To My Readers

Well, darlin's, this is it. My very first book baby. And the fact that you picked it up means the whole wide world to me.

Thank you for taking a chance on a brand-new author. Every page you turn, every review you leave, every time you recommend my book to a friend, you're helping me build this dream brick by brick. That kind of trust is something I'll never take for granted.

So from the bottom of my sweet-tea-fueled, book-lovin' heart: thank you for making this debut more than just a checkmark on my bucket list. Thank you for makin' it the start of a whole new adventure.

I sure hope you'll stick around because this is just the beginning.

ABOUT THE AUTHOR

I grew up among the citrus trees and salt air of Florida, where stories were as common as thunderstorms and family ties run deep.

Raised in a blue-collar family with roots stretching back to orange groves, I learned early on that resilience and heart were the cornerstones of any good life (and any good story). Summers were spent barefoot, climbing trees and riding bikes down dirt roads, while the grown-ups swapped stories over potluck dinners and folding chairs in the backyard.

Books were a constant escape and a secret dream. With a lineage full of storytellers, veterans, and caretakers, it was only natural that one day I would start weaving tales of love, strength, and second chances. Drawing on the quiet dignity of working-class life, and the romance tucked between everyday moments, I write stories that feel like home: warm, genuine, and always a little sun-kissed.

Though the name on the cover might belong to one, the voice behind the pen is shaped by many generations of grit, grace, and just a touch of Southern charm.

xoxo,
TC